Alex Drakos
House on Fire

Mallory Monroe

AUSTIN BROOK PUBLISHING

This novel is a work of fiction. All characters are fictitious. Any similarities to ayone living or dead are completely accidental. The specific mention of known places or venues are not meant to be exact replicas of those places, but they are purposely embellished or imagined for the story's sake. The cover art are models. They are not actual characters.

THE RAGS TO ROMANCE SERIES

STANDALONE BOOKS

IN PUBLICATION ORDER:

1. BOBBY SINATRA: IN ALL THE
WRONG PLACES

2. BOONE & CHARLY: SECOND
CHANCE LOVE

3. PLAIN JANE EVANS AND THE
BILLIONAIRE

4. GENTLEMAN JAMES AND GINA

5. MONTY & LaSHAY: RESCUE ME

6. TONY SINATRA: IF LOVING YOU IS
WRONG

7. WHEN A MAN LOVES A WOMAN

8. THE DUKE AND THE MAID

9. BOONE AND CHARLY: UPSIDE
DOWN LOVE

10. HOOD RILEY AND THE ICE MAN

11. RECRUITED BY THE BILLIONAIRE

12. ABANDONED HEARTS

13. HOOD RILEY AND THE ICE MAN 2:

JUST WHEN I NEEDED YOU MOST

MALLORY MONROE SERIES:

THE RENO GABRINI/MOB BOSS SERIES (22 BOOKS)

THE SAL GABRINI SERIES (12 BOOKS)

THE TOMMY GABRINI SERIES (11 BOOKS)

THE MICK SINATRA SERIES (15 BOOKS)

THE BIG DADDY SINATRA SERIES (7 BOOKS)

THE TEDDY SINATRA SERIES (5 BOOKS)

THE TREVOR REESE SERIES (3 BOOKS)

THE AMELIA SINATRA SERIES (2 BOOKS)

THE BRENT SINATRA SERIES (1 BOOK)

THE ALEX DRAKOS SERIES (10 BOOKS)

THE OZ DRAKOS SERIES (2 BOOKS)

THE MONK PALETTI SERIES (2 BOOKS)

THE PRESIDENT'S GIRLFRIEND SERIES (8 BOOKS)

THE PRESIDENT'S BOYFRIEND SERIES (1 BOOK)

THE RAGS TO ROMANCE SERIES (12 BOOKS)

GIRLS ON THE RUN: A GABRINI VALENTINE

STANDALONE BOOKS:

DANIEL'S GIRL

(*Brand new version updated and expanded*)

ROMANCING MO RYAN

MAEBELLE MARIE

LOVING HER SOUL MATE

LOVING THE HEAD MAN

TABLE OF CONTENTS

CHAPTER ONE

CHAPTER TWO

CHAPTER THREE

CHAPTER FOUR

CHAPTER FIVE

CHAPTER SIX

CHAPTER SEVEN

CHAPTER EIGHT

CHAPTER NINE

CHAPTER TEN

CHAPTER ELEVEN

CHAPTER TWELVE

CHAPTER THIRTEEN

CHAPTER FOURTEEN

CHAPTER FIFTEEN

CHAPTER SIXTEEN

CHAPTER SEVENTEEN

CHAPTER EIGHTEEN

CHAPTER NINETEEN

CHAPTER TWENTY

CHAPTER TWENTY-ONE

CHAPTER TWENTY-TWO

CHAPTER TWENTY-THREE

CHAPTER TWENTY-FOUR

CHAPTER TWENTY-FIVE

CHAPTER TWENTY-SIX

CHAPTER TWENTY-SEVEN

CHAPTER TWENTY-EIGHT

CHAPTER TWENTY-NINE

CHAPTER THIRTY

CHAPTER THIRTY-ONE

CHAPTER THIRTY-TWO

CHAPTER THIRTY-THREE

CHAPTER THIRTY-FOUR

CHAPTER THIRTY-FIVE

CHAPTER THIRTY-SIX

CHAPTER THIRTY-SEVEN

CHAPTER THIRTY-EIGHT

CHAPTER THIRTY-NINE

CHAPTER FORTY

EPILOGUE

CHAPTER ONE

"Oh this is lovely." Lucinda was nodding her approval as Kari pulled a super-short bodycon dress from the dress rack. "It will look so cute on you."

"If you wanna look like a ho," said Faye, "then that'll do the trick."

Lucinda gave Faye a hard glare. "You would know my darling," she said, as she jerked her blonde hair backwards.

Kari ignored her two closest friends and pulled another dress off the rack. They were all supposed to be out shopping that day, but for some reason both of them were following Kari all around the store. And neither one of them were hesitating to give her their opinions on everything she so much as glanced.

"That's cute too," Lucinda said as she

ALEX DRAKOS: HOUSE ON FIRE

saw the latest dress Kari was eyeing. "Or do you have a complaint about this one too?"

Lucinda was talking to Faye, but a good-looking man was looking Faye up and down as men usually did, and Faye was giving him a once-over too. With her flawless dark skin, beautiful face, and smoking-hot body, Faye was always considered the most beautiful girl in any room she entered. And she played to her strengths.

"Faye? Faye? Can you stop looking at some man for two seconds and help Kari."

"Why would you think I need her help? I know how to pick out my own clothes."

Lucinda looked doubtfully at Kari. "When was the last time you bought anything approximately resembling clothes, Karena?"

"What are you talking about? I just got this I have on," Kari said, glancing down at the form-fitting dress she wore.

"Did you go out and buy it yourself personally, or did Alex have it flown in from Paris or Milan or wherever he gets your clothes from?"

Kari realized it had been a while since she last went shopping for herself. Or even wore an off-the-rack outfit. But she quickly dismissed it. "I've never been into clothes like that anyway," she said.

When the wife of Faye's admirer grabbed

her husband by the arm, glowered at Faye, and then dragged him away from her, she smiled. And looked at Lucinda. "Now what were you saying?"

"I was saying that dress Kari's looking at is cute."

"It's cute," said Faye, "if you're going to your fiftieth-class reunion. Or maybe to church."

"Church," said Lucinda. "Now where did I hear that name before?"

"Ah fuck you, Lou!"

Kari and Lucinda both were shocked by Faye's change in tone. Kari especially was surprise. "Really, Faye? Is that what we're doing? Talking that disrespectfully to our friends?"

"She's always pulling that bullshit," Faye responded. "She knows my divorce just became final. She knows it's still a sore spot for me. But yet in still she twists that knife every chance she gets."

"I was just joking Faye, my goodness. You mentioned church. Your last name used to be Church. I thought it was funny."

"Well it's not," Faye said to Lucinda. "White woman always got jokes." Then she looked at her longtime white friend. "But not at my expense," she added.

Lucinda had no idea what race would

11

have had to do with it. But that was Faye too. "You are such a drama queen," she said.

"Even I'm still calling you Faye Church," Kari said as her phone began to ring, "instead of Faye Marshall. We're all adjusting to your new normal." When Kari saw that it was her son, she answered the call. "Hey J, what's up?"

"Daddy's home, Ma."

Did Kari hear him right? "Now? Or he's coming home?"

"He's home right now. And he's asking for you. He wants to see you."

"I'm on my way," Kari said happily, and ended the call.

"What's wrong?" Faye asked her.

"Alex is back in town."

"And?"

"And I need to go home and see my husband. I haven't seen him or heard from him in over three weeks."

When Kari slipped and admitted that truth, saying it out loud made her realize how crazy it sounded. She looked at Faye and Lucinda. She could tell it sounded crazy to them too.

"Hold up. Your husband has been out of town for three straight weeks," said Faye, "and he hasn't gotten in touch with you in all that time?"

"And you're breaking your neck to go be with him?" asked Lucinda. "Are you serious, Kare?"

"It's not like that. When he's negotiating deals he has to stay focused. He can't get caught up in drama back home. That's all that's about."

"But come on, Kare!" Faye could hardly believe it. "What if you have an emergency? What if you need to contact him? What if you want to know if he's okay?"

"Then I contact one of his assistants and they'll have him phone me right away."

Faye was floored. "One of his assistants?" She shook her head and looked at Lucinda as if Kari had lost her mind. "I can't," she said.

Kari knew exactly why they were reacting the way they were. Spoken out loud, it did sound nuts! The old Kari Grant, the one they met when she first came to town and started her own maid service, wouldn't take crap from any man and they knew it. And they couldn't reconcile the old Kari Grant with the new Kari Drakos. But their focus on Alex not calling her was the least of her worries. She understood his energy when he was handling his business. He had a ritual and he was sticking to it. His constant absences was the major issue for Kari.

That was the big-ass elephant in the room. But her friends were more concerned about phone calls.

"I'll talk to y'all later," she said as she headed for the exit. She was anxious to see Alex again, she didn't care what they thought.

But they had reawakened in Kari what had been simmering deep within her for a long time: Alex was gone too damn much. He had gotten better. Much better. Then he started sliding right back into those same old habits once again. And when Alex slid, he *slid*!

But Kari knew one thing for certain: she was tired of tolerating it. And the longer she allowed it, the longer he was going to keep doing it. He wasn't ever going to change if she didn't force the issue. But at what price? Because she knew there would be a price to pay to her own sense of self if she continued to allow him to keep neglecting his responsibilities to her and their children. But she also knew there would be an even greater price to pay to their marriage if she was ready to make that change, but he wasn't.

Roz Sinatra warned her not to let it slide. And so did Trina Gabrini. Jenay told her it would be a disaster if she didn't nip it in the bud. But she was so busy doing her own thing that she didn't notice how bad it had gotten until it was beyond bad. And her girlfriends were worried about phone calls. That was the least of Kari's worries.

She left that store without looking back.

But as she walked out, Lucinda looked at Faye. "What's happened to Kari? I don't recognize that girl with all of this bowing down to Alex bullcrap. What happened?"

"She loves her husband. That's what happened. She's no longer the Kari Grant we used to know. She's not that girl anymore. She's all Kari Drakos now. And that's a different chick altogether."

Lucinda shook her head. "Men. They'll be the death of women yet. I'm so glad I'm divorced and don't have to answer to any man anymore."

"You?" Faye smiled as if she couldn't agree more. "Me too, girl. Me too!"

But neither one of them, in the privacy of their own hearts, meant a word of it.

CHAPTER TWO

Alex Drakos was slouched down on the sofa inside his penthouse apartment that sat atop The Drakos Hotel and Casino in Apple Valley, Florida with his son Jordan on one side of him, and his daughter Angela on the other side of him. Both of them were leaned against him as if they were keeping him put until their mother could get home. He'd been gone so often that they rarely got to see him. And when they did see him? It was an event.

Alex's younger brother Oz Drakos and his wife Gloria Sinatra-Drakos, along with their daughter, were also in the house. Oz was seated in the chair while Gloria was seated on the floor between his legs, with their daughter asleep on her lap. Everybody was happy Alex was home. It was like a big deal around the place whenever he got back. But they all could tell he was bone tired.

But Jordan was curious about his uncle's response to the unruly crowd he was talking about that had visited the casino downstairs. "What I want to know is what did you do about it, Uncle Oz? You have to treat those frat boys delicately you know."

"I treated them delicate alright. I singlehandedly tossed each and every one of those clowns out on their asses."

"Oz, there are children here," warned Gloria.

"Out on their butts, okay?" Oz responded to his wife in a tone that made Gloria look away. Ever since they said I do, it had been a rollercoaster ride of a marriage for both of them.

But Oz didn't seem to notice. "They may get away with those antics at Dreston or Florida State or FAM or wherever they went to school, but they weren't tearing up my casino."

"They don't go to Dreston." Jordan was a student at Dreston. "We Dreston men know how to behave ourselves. And besides, Uncle Oz, you said *my* casino. Don't you mean Dad's casino?"

"Oh yeah. Him too," said Oz, and everybody laughed.

Alex smiled and looked at Jordan. Although he adopted him when he married Jordan's mother, they were closer than any biological father/son could have ever been. "How's school?"

"It's good. The college debate tournament starts next week and lasts for three months every Saturday. Then there are the playoffs and championship. We're determined to win not just State, but the nationals this year."

"Have they selected team officers yet?"

"Guess who's team captain?" said Oz proudly.

Alex looked at Jordan. "You're team captain?"

Jordan smiled. "Yes sir. I'm the first African-American to be captain of the debating team in Dreston's 112-year history."

"Jordan's smart!" said Angela with a grin, and they all laughed.

But Alex was serious. He saw Jordan as the heir to his empire. And he was proving his worthiness of such an elevation on a daily basis. Alex placed an arm around Jordan. "Congratulations son. My businesses will be in excellent hands one day." Then Alex added: "If I still have businesses."

Oz looked at his big brother. "Negotiations stalled again?"

"Not stalled. Stopped. Ended."

"On what terms?"

"Every term. We're light years away from each other. It's no deal."

Oz shook his head. "I don't know how you do it, brother. I would have turned that place out had I traveled that long, and stayed that long, with no results. They would feel what they did to me."

"I believe they'll return to the table once they realize the error of their ways. I was bought in to try and pull it over the finish line. And we were close. Until they got greedy. Until they thought I wouldn't walk away."

"You, brother? They don't know you if they thought you wouldn't walk away. They don't know you at all!"

Then Alex let out a yawn and stretched his arms. "I am one tired individual," he said as he began standing on his feet. "I hate to break up the band, but I'm going to go lie down for a few."

Jordan and Angela, as if on cue, got up, too, and began to follow their father toward the stairs. Oz and Gloria saw them. They knew how infrequent they got to see Alex lately. And it broke their hearts.

"Guys," said Oz, and Jordan and Angela looked at him. "Let him get some rest. He's just going upstairs. He's not going to jump out any windows and get away again."

Jordan felt particularly exposed and pulled his baby sister back. He was a college kid now, for crying out loud, in the very prestigious, very private, very exclusive Dreston University, some twenty miles outside of Apple Valley, and he was following his old man toe-to-toe? But even though they stopped walking

19

when Oz made his statement, they both watched as Alex made his way up the stairs. All of Jordan's friends hated being around their fathers. But Jordan loved being around his dad. His dad just wasn't around much anymore.

Gloria elbowed Oz on his leg. "Ouch!" Oz said, until she looked at him and then gave a slight nod toward the children. And Oz, who missed his brother, too, and had been watching his retreat up those stairs as well, sprang into action. "Don't you want to hear more about your uncle's incredible escapades? I admit I'm no Alexio." Then he smiled his charming smile that he knew they loved, and flung his long hair out of his handsome face. "But I'm his baby brother. I'm the next best thing."

It did its' job. Jordan, with his protective arms on Angela's tiny shoulders, walked with her over to the sofa and they sat down and listened as Oz told them more about the daily drama that was the hallmark of the casino downstairs.

But less than ten minutes later, Kari walked in.

As soon as Kari made her way through the foyer and into the living room area, Angela jumped up and ran to her mother. "Mommy!" she yelled as she ran. "Daddy's home, Mommy! Daddy's home!"

"Is he?" Kari smiled a smile that Oz and Gloria could tell was bittersweet as she grabbed her young daughter into a big bear hug. The fact that Angie was happy that her father was home was sweet to all of them. The fact that both of her children looked as if they, like her, were worried that it wouldn't be for long was going to one day turn her into a very bitter woman. But that was if she allowed it to continue. If Oz was a betting man, *and he was*, his money was on Kari putting an ax to it before she allowed it to continue.

Jordan was happy to see her too. She was the only one who had the balls to handle their father the way he needed to be handled. Now their father would have an anchor to help keep him in place, was his thought. Although lately he felt that his mother was dropping the ball too.

Kari looked at Jordan. There used to be a time when it was just the two of them. It sometimes used to feel as if they could read each other's mind just from the expression on their faces. She could tell what that look on his face was saying. He was happy to see his dad, but worried too. "Hey, J, what's up?"

"Nothing. Dad was down here with us. But he left us."

Kari almost frowned. But she knew

Jordan. He had a flare, sometimes, for the dramatic.

"He's upstairs, Kari," said Oz. "Don't mind that son of yours who fails to mention that his father is bone tired. He's upstairs resting for a minute, that's all."

Kari nodded. One side of her was on Jordan's side. His ass just got back. He could rest later. Spend some quality time with his children first! But the other side of her was so happy Alex was home that she wasn't sure which side would win out.

She was about to find out. She managed to separate herself from Angela, and slowly made her way upstairs.

CHAPTER THREE

Alex was lying on top of the bed, still in his well-tailored suit of clothes, including his big-ass dress shoes, she noticed, as she stood at the open double doors of their French Provincial-styled bedroom. What pissed her off wasn't that he was lying in bed, which was fine. She was certain he probably was extremely tired. But that he was lying in bed *on his phone* was what did it for her.

"Too tired to spend time with our children," she said, "but not too tired to text?"

Alex looked up when he heard her voice. And although it was a critical voice, his heartbeat quickened just seeing her again. It was that look she had about her that did it for him. That Kari look: sometimes harsh, sometimes incredibly uncompromising, but also a very tender and vulnerable look that she carried with her everywhere she went. She'd never know how much he missed her. And needed her. "Hey," he said as he sat his phone on the nightstand beside their bed.

But she just stood there, looking sexy as hell to Alex with her hair dropped mistakenly across her right eye and that dress he purchased for her in Paris gorgeously tight across her ample breasts and flat stomach. And although she was very slender, she had curves. He was getting aroused just looking at her again. No woman turned him on the way Kari did. And he knew it wasn't just her smoking body. It was *her*. He never knew how deep love could go until he met Kari. "Close and lock those doors," he said when she didn't move on her own. "And come to me."

Kari remained where she stood. They should have been addressing their problems, not locking themselves away in the bedroom. But that was the issue. Alex didn't seem able to see the magnitude of the problem, and how it was affecting his family, at all. And that was why Kari got directly to the point. "You have got to spend more time with our children, Alex," she said to him.

Alex didn't expect a lecture, and a part of him didn't like that she had that lecturing tone, but he knew she was telling the truth. "Understood."

"I don't give a flying fuck if you understand it or don't understand it. You have got to do it. It's not about you understanding that you need to do it. It's not about you talking about doing it. You have got to do it. They need you. Jordan needs you."

Alex let out a harsh exhale. Kari could tell he was pissed. But she also knew Alex was a fair man, and if he was faltering, and she pointed it out to him, he wouldn't deny it.

And he didn't. But he did try to explain it away, which only pissed off Kari. "I'll do my best," he said. "You know I will. But I'm working on all cylinders as it is, Karena. We've had a recession, a weak recovery, and now we're being plunged right back into an even more dire recession. Businesses are closing left and right. The only thing that's keeping us afloat are the partnerships I've been able to garner. And now we need even more partners to stay afloat. And Moody's just this morning predicted that this recession could last years, Kari. Not months, but years. And I've got to navigate this ship. This shit don't sail on its own. I'm doing the best I can."

Kari could see the strain in Alex's eyes even from across the room. And she understood what he was saying. She heard all of those prognosticators this morning too. But the children had to come first. "Even if you're doing your best," she said, "you have got to do more for the children." Then she added: "And for me."

Alex stared at her. He was neglecting the shit out of her, too, and he knew it. He had hoped that things would have settled back down by now. But they seemed to be picking up steam again. And he knew that level of neglect wasn't going to be tolerated. Not by a woman like Kari. Nor should it be. But he couldn't split himself in half.

He nodded his head. "I'll do more," he promised.

It wasn't good enough. Because Kari knew Alex. They were just words until the next crisis hit and he had to take off again. But she wasn't going to let the perfect become the enemy of the good. He was home right now. They had him with them right now. She was going to take advantage of that.

She closed and locked the door. Then she walked over to her dressing table and sat her bag down, kicked off her heels, dropped her keys, and then made her way to the bed. She was about to sit on the edge of the bed, but Alex pulled her on top of him. And when he wrapped his big arms around her small body, she immediately felt secure.

"Hey," he said to her again with that smile on his face where barely visible crow's feet wrinkles appeared on the sides of his eyes and his tiredness showed with slight bagginess beneath his eyes. But he still was the sexiest man alive to Kari, and to most women on the face of this earth, even with those imperfections. She could already feel herself melting in his arms.

"Hey," she said to him. And as he placed his hand on the back of her head and moved her mouth closer to his mouth, and when he looked into her eyes with that hooded, lustful look that always did it for Kari, she closed her eyes in anticipation of what she knew was going to be exactly what the doctor ordered.

And as soon as their lips touched, it was over for both of them. Any conversations and concerns, and even Kari's anger at Alex, dissipated away like dew in the morning. And suddenly they were all feeling now. They were all into each other, and not their less-than ideal circumstances now. And when Alex's dick began to hardened to steel-like proportions beneath her, and he began to moan in her mouth as if what she was giving him was the best kiss he'd ever had, she was a goner too.

It took no time for them to be naked on that bed and for Alex to have Kari on her back and his big body on top of her. To her ever-loving delight he was sucking her breasts for minutes on end, as if he couldn't get enough of them, and Kari was groaning and moving around on the bed to the magnificent feelings his mastery caused her to experience.

And when he moved further down, between her legs, she arched so high that Alex had to lift his head to stay with her. Because he wasn't letting up. For minutes on end, he wouldn't ease up. And Kari was loving every second.

And when he did finally ease up and turned her onto her stomach, and when he entered her from the back with a thrust that caused her to arch that tight ass he loved so much, she let out a sigh so guttural that it lasted a long, wonderful time.

Alex was fucking her hard and wasn't trying to go easy. The squeeze of her tight ass as he banged her made him even more determined to put it on her long, hard, and right. And when her small hands grabbed hold of their satin sheets as if she was trying to claw away from the electricity they were generating, that only made him bang harder. And she was moaning deeper the harder he banged. It was the way they loved it. Not all the time. Only when they had been without each other for an appreciable amount of time did they need it to be the way Alex was putting it on her. This was one of those times.

For nearly an hour they were going at it. From Kari on her stomach, to Kari on her back, to Alex on his back and Kari right back on top of him, they weren't trying to do anything but make each other feel better than they'd felt in weeks. And it worked.

And when they came, they went hard there too. Until Alex poured into Kari and Kari was so overfilled with his cum that she started having rolling orgasms, not just one. And he was hanging right in there with her. Until neither one of them could hang another second, and they collapsed into each other's arms.

And it worked again. They forgot their troubles, and held on.

CHAPTER FOUR

The next morning, Jordan and Angie, seated in the kitchen at the center island, were pleased to find that their father, in a pristine white shirt with his suit coat off, was still at home and preparing breakfast for them.

They talked about everything, including Jordan's upcoming debate season, and his role as captain of the team. Alex equated it with his role, once upon a time, as captain of his soccer team back in his native Greece. "Treat every teammate," he advised Jordan, "as if they were the most important component to the success of the team. And guess what?"

"They'll start acting the part?"

Alex nodded. "Exactly right," he said as he sat plates of food in front of his children.

He continued with his advice as Angela ate up the food while Jordan ate up his father's wisdom. He knew Alex wanted him to helm the Drakos Corporation someday, and he was determined to be fully prepared and ready when that day came. He pushed his glasses up on his face and listened far more than he talked.

Alex talked and fixed himself a breakfast plate too. But before he started plating Kari's breakfast, he looked at his Cartier watch. "J, go check on your mother. She got up when I got up." They even showered together, with Alex fucking her once again in that shower while they were at it. "She should have been down by now."

"Yes, sir," Jordan said and hurried out of the kitchen, across the living room, and toward the front stairs.

But when he got to the stairs, he saw his mother standing on the third from the bottom step. She wasn't moving. Which looked odd to him. "Ma? What's wrong?"

He realized that his mother wasn't just standing there, but was staring at something by the front door. He turned toward his opposite side, which was their foyer, and that was when he saw it too. Alex's suitcase and briefcase, with his suitcoat flapped over both, were sitting in the foyer undoubtedly waiting for his man to take to the car. They knew that scene like the back of their hands. And although Kari was shocked, Jordan was pissed.

"Again? He just got home!" Then he shook his head. "I knew it was too good to be true," he said as he made his way back into the kitchen. Kari, disappointed too, followed him.

But Jordan wasn't sticking around. "Come on, Ang," he said as he grabbed his bookbag by the side of his stool, "we're late for school."

"What do you mean you're late?" Alex asked. "You haven't finished your breakfast yet."

But Jordan only looked at his father. And Angela, a very perspective child, looked at her brother. And she could see him staring daggers at their father. And if her brain was telling her to pick a side, she chose Jordan's side. Of their whole family, he was the one that made her feel safest. He was the one she could count on the most. And she didn't question it. She grabbed her bookbag, too, gave her mother and her father a kiss, and then left. Jordan had already gone.

Although Alex had a good idea what was going on, he was reluctant to face it. "What's his problem?" he asked Kari.

Kari looked at him as she stood at the center island. "Really? That's what we're doing? We're playing dumb now?"

"Don't talk to me like that."

"I'll talk to you any way I *got*damn well please!" Kari was fired up. "You're leaving again?"

"I have no choice."

Kari shook her head. "Unbelievable. What we talked about last night didn't mean shit

32

to you."

"They came back to the negotiating table. We've got a deal that I've got to close."

"Why do *you* have to close it?"

"Because it's top to top. Their chairman is showing up, which means I have to show up. If I don't and send one of my people instead, it would be such a massive level of disrespect that it could derail the talks again. And I'm not taking that chance."

Kari lifted her head back and shook her head again. Alex could see the anguish in her beautiful eyes, and he was sorry that he was the source of that distress.

Kari looked at him. They were always caught between a rock and a hard place. But what could she do? He was singing his doomsday song again where only he and he alone could save the company. How could she fight against that scenario? "Where this time?"

"Chicago. I'm hoping for a quick turnaround. I should be back tomorrow."

"Until the next time?" Kari asked it and looked at Alex as if she was daring him to lie to her.

"Yes," he said.

He didn't lie, but it still hurt. He could see it in her eyes. "When will there not be a next time, Alex? We can't keep going on this way.

We were doing great. You were doing your part and it was beautiful. Then I wake up one day and realize it's off the rails again. What happened?"

"An unexpected recession happened, Kare. Nobody expected the U.S. to get out of one recession and get right back into another one. And one even harsher than the last one. We withstood the last one. That was why I wasn't traveling as much. It wasn't hard-hitting my industry. But this one is different. It's coming straight for businesses like mine. And it's digging in for the long haul. I've got to stay ahead of this beast or it will take me under. That's what happened. I would stay if I could. You know I would."

Kari exhaled. Because she knew he would if he could. He wasn't lying. That was the only reason she was putting up with his shit.

But she had her limits. "Carve out time for your family, Alex, and I mean that. If you expect to keep one."

Alex stared at her. He knew she was only saying that out of anger. But it still pissed him off. He needed her to be there for him right now, not get on the complaint bandwagon too. But he held his tongue. Because he knew it wasn't fair. Kari was his ride or die and had been throughout their entire time together. But for her to threaten him with leaving and taking their children with her was a low blow.

"I've got a plane to catch," he said, and headed for the foyer.

Kari leaned her head back again. And what angered her wasn't the fact that he was leaving. But the fact that she didn't want him to leave like that.

And she did it. She ran into the foyer just as he had put on his suitcoat and was picking up his briefcase. And she rounded the corner and stood there. Alex turned and looked at her. And when he saw that look of regret in her eyes that matched the regret he felt in his heart, he sat his briefcase back down. And went to Kari. He pulled her into his arms and they kissed. It was just supposed to be a simple kiss to put them back on the same page again. But their emotions got in the way.

And before they knew it they had forgotten their troubles once again and were fucking in the foyer.

And when it was over, Kari's panties were on one side of the foyer, while she was seated on the Queen Anne table on the opposite side of the foyer looking just like the woman Alex remembered the first time he met her in that diner. And he smiled. And kissed her again. And Kari smiled back and grabbed a heap of her gorgeous hair and slung it behind her back while Alex zipped up his pants. He was about to leave and she had pleased her man again. And yet they were staring hungrily at each other once again.

And Alex couldn't just leave. He moved up to her and placed his hands on either side of her beautiful face. "Come hell or high water," he said to her, "I'll be back no later than tomorrow. Okay?"

She nodded her assent. As if she hadn't already assented by fucking him. And then he left.

But he kept his promise. He was back by noon the very next day. And Kari and the children rejoiced. They had him safe and home and he was thrilled to be there.

But by the end of that same week, another must-do had to be done, and he was on the road again. But like a drug addict, Kari was too hooked on Alex to give him up. She and the children were too hooked on Alex period to even think about making any kind of ultimatums to him. And they all let it slide.

And slide.

And slide.

Until one day, three months later, Kari would come to the ultimate realization that they had let it slide to such an extent that if something didn't change and change in a hurry, they were all, as a family, going to slide right over a cliff.

CHAPTER FIVE

THREE MONTHS LATER

Jordan entered The Drakos and decided to take the stairs instead. It was more flights than he'd ever climbed before, but he lumbered on. Running at first, then jogging, and now he was barely walking up the final few flights. And when he entered the penthouse, he was ready to crash.

But his mother was hurrying into the foyer and grabbing her Versace bag and keys from off of the Queen Anne table. "About time," she said. "I need you to watch Ang."

"Where are you headed?"

"Dinner. Have you eaten?"

"I told you I was going out with Matty and the guys. Yeah, I ate. What about Ang?"

"She ate too. She's on the sofa on her phone. And don't give her any sweets. It's almost her bedtime."

"Yes ma'am."

Then Kari looked at Jordan. "How did it go?"

"We placed."

"Placed what? Third? Second?"

"We won."

Kari smiled and squeezed his chin. "That's great, J. And I'm sure every one of the members of that debating team attributes your leadership for their success."

"I'm sure they don't," said Jordan. "They attribute themselves. As do I. I wouldn't have it any other way."

"Spoken like a great leader," said Kari. "Why are you breathing so heavily?"

"I took the stairs."

"All of them?"

"All of them."

"Why?"

"I need exercise. I'm getting fat."

"Boy bye!" said Kari. Her son was not getting fat in any way, shape, or form. But maybe to some special girl he was? "I'll be back," she said as she wrapped a scarf around her neck and began to leave.

"Heard from Dad?" Jordan suddenly asked her. It was a topic always brewing beneath the surface.

Kari hated whenever Jordan asked that question, because the answer was always the same. She, instead, kissed him on the cheek and took off.

Jordan locked the door and then leaned against it. He was drained.

And he knew what the answer to his question was. He knew it before he asked it. But even in his absence Alex took all of the oxygen out of their home.

But he wasn't going to dwell on it. He pushed himself away from the door and went to see about his beloved baby sister.

CHAPTER SIX

Across the pond, in historic Athens, Greece, Alex's limousine stopped in front of the mammoth Drakos Corporate headquarters building and the bodyguard hopped out of the front passenger seat and opened the back passenger door. The chief operating officer, Dave Pantanzis, and the chief financial officer, Walter Vokos, were waiting out front to welcome the boss. Although they both were Greek, they spoke flawless English.

Alex stepped out of the limo, buttoned his tailored suit, and made his way across the sidewalk to two of the men responsible for the day-to-day operations of his company's European southeastern sector.

"Alex, welcome," said Dave as he smilingly extended his hand.

"Is that what it's called?" Alex asked as he walked past Dave's outstretched hand and headed for the entrance. He was not in any handshaking mood. Not after the report he'd received. He headed inside of his corporate building.

Dave and Walter looked at each other, understanding now that the wrath of Drakos had arrived, and hurried in behind him.

Alex didn't say a word until he entered the boardroom and stood at the head of the table. The Drakos Corporation in Europe operated from sectors in various regions of the continent. All of the executives in his southeast sector were assembled. Dave and Walter hurried to take their seats too.

Alex opened his suit coat, placed his hands on his hips, and didn't mince words. "Who fucked up?" he asked them. "I want names and I want dates."

Everybody stiffened. And looked at Walter, the CFO.

"Sir," said Walter, moving up in his seat, "it's not that simple. She was able to access all of our systems. She was moving money when we didn't even know there was money to be moved."

"When we discovered the breach," Dave added, " it was already over. Galani Masarkis was nowhere to be found."

But Alex wasn't buying it. "You expect me to believe that bullshit?"

Walter seemed caught off guard. "Yes, sir. It's the truth, sir."

"What's the final total?"

That was the number nobody wanted to verbalize. But Walter knew he had to because

Alex was looking directly at him. "Eighty-three percent of our working capital is missing, sir."

Alex frowned. "*Eighty-three percent?*"

Walter looked grief-stricken. But he nodded his head. "Yes, sir."

Alex was so beside himself with anger that he walked away from the table. But then his anger unleashed and he hurried back up to that table, pulled out his fully loaded Glock, and sat it on the table. Everybody in that room sat up straight. They knew all about Alex's past in the Greek mafia. Some of them had come from the same past. They knew what he was capable of. And in that moment, he wanted them to know it.

"You have thirty days. Thirty days, gentlemen, to restore my corporation's financial health back to where it was the day a dime went missing, and you have thirty days to restore Galani as the CEO of this sector."

"But sir," said Dave, "she's the one who caused this crisis."

"Bullshit!" yelled the usually cool Alex. "That's bullshit. There is no scenario where I'm going to let you put this theft at her feet. I handpicked her for a reason. She steered us back from the brink when Dimitri Kalashnik tried to take us down. This sector outperformed every sector I have. And that was because of

Galani. And now you expect me to believe she suddenly woke up one day and pulled that same shit herself? Whoever in this room thought I was going to fall for that forgot who they were dealing with."

Then Alex's look turned hard and cold. "I will kill every motherfucker at this table if my money and my CEO are not restored in thirty days. And if anybody has harmed a hair on Galani's head, I'll kill you for that too. That's who you're dealing with."

Alex didn't like playing that gangster shit he spent a lifetime getting as far away from as he possibly could. But stealing eighty percent of that sector's entire revenue stream was a gangster move. He was matching the moment.

He stared at them a few seconds longer. Then he picked up his Glock. "Thirty days, gentlemen," he said, and then left the room.

Everybody let out a harsh exhale. Then Walter shook his head. "I told you it wouldn't work!"

"It will work if we stick together," said Dave. "No divisions. No second-guessing. He doesn't know shit, Walt, he's just talking! We're in this together and we will be successful if we don't get stupid. Everybody do their part and we'll make our beautiful plan a reality. I told you he would come at us sideways. Didn't I tell you that? But he's got nothing. He's just trying us. We've got to stick together no matter what!"

"And when those thirty days are up?" asked Walter. "What then, Dave? What then?"

He was panicking. Everybody could see it. But Dave smiled. Nobody was going to see him sweat. "Lots can happen in thirty days, my friend. A lot *will* happen in thirty days. That's in the plan too. All you need to do is shut your mouth and trust the process. Drakos has been our puppet master for as long as some of us can remember. He hired us and gave us this chance, but he never respected us as his equals. We are the ones who made this sector successful, not him. Not Galani. We are the ones! But all his life has been the same thing: whatever Alexio Drakos wants, Alexio Drakos gets. And he never considers anybody else. Look at what he did to his own son. Look at what he did to Cate. They decided to take for themselves a few dollars that he should have simply given to them, and what does he do? He phoned the police on them. On his own children! He drove his poor, unfortunate son to kill himself. Cate ended up in prison. Remember all of that? He brought shame on Greece. I will never forget it!"

Although everybody else at the table were nodding their heads in remembrance of that dark time too, Walter wasn't one of them. "It wasn't a few dollars," he pointed out. "It was millions of dollars they stole from their own father."

"What was a few million to Alexio Drakos? He could have overlooked it. Those children were all he had and he was willing to throw them away based on what? Money he didn't even need?" Dave shook his head. "That is why we had to take what I feel is rightfully ours, and take it big. To get his attention."

"And now that we have his attention," said Walter, "he will kill us if we do not replace every dime of his money. He said so himself."

"And he's telling the truth," said Dave. "He will absolutely hunt each one of us down like dogs in the street and kill us one by one. But as I said, a lot can happen in thirty days. Like I said, a lot *will* happen in thirty days."

"You also said he would never suspect us," said Walter. "And we were the first he suspected!"

Everybody looked to their fearless leader Dave Pantanzis. Because Walter was right.

"He was a lot sharper than I perhaps gave him credit for," said Dave. "But what else did I tell you? Contingencies are always a part of any plan I hatch. And we have many contingencies."

"But you said he will kill us if we don't replace that money. What difference does any contingency make if he's going to handle each one of us?"

"Because we have thirty days," said Dave. "And when we finish handling him, finally handling the great Alexio Drakos, those of us in this room and that lost revenue will be the absolute least of his worries. In fact, when it is all said and done, he will have no worries at all. None."

Dave smiled again. Only it was a reptilian smile. The kind that reminded them all he was just as gangster as Drakos. "Trust the process. Follow my lead. And we not only will be rich and can finally enjoy that money we rightfully took for ourselves, but we will own the entirety of his European conglomerate. Not just the southeastern sector. All of the sectors." Then any hint of a smile left Dave's face. "We stick firmly and entirely and unabashedly to the plan. Period!"

And everybody else, except for Walter Vokos, were relieved that their leader was thinking ahead, and wasn't going to take any setback for granted.

But after the meeting, as they all rose and began voicing their relief that things just might work out after all, Dave glanced over at Frank

Savalas, the sector's security chief, who was also at the table. If they were going to keep it together to get to the other side, they both knew what they had to do.

That was why, when Walter Vokos left the room, Dave nodded at Frank. And Frank, who had his own gangster pedigree, left the room too.

CHAPTER SEVEN

Faye Marshall laughed so hard she started coughing. "You stupid!" she said happily to her dinner companion.

They were in Piper's, an upscale restaurant in the very upscale Apple Valley, Florida. Diallo Koffi, her dinner companion, grinned as he took another sip of his wine. "Humorous," he said in his heavy Nigerian-English accent, "but never stupid."

"It's an American expression," said Faye. "It signifies my appreciation of your silliness. To look at you nobody would view you as a jokester. I know I didn't when I first laid eyes on you."

"You *laid eyes* on me, did you?"

Faye laughed again. "Another expression."

"But was it my face that you were laying these eyes upon, or something else?"

Good comeback, Faye thought. "I was looking slightly down from the face, yes, I'll admit it. But then I eventually, *after several hours*, looked up at the face too."

Diallo grinned. "You are a jokester yourself."

"But seriously, Dee, all jokes aside. Have you ever thought of settling down?"

"Have you?"

"Been there, done that. I told you I was divorced. I was the wife of Mr. Benjamin "Benny" Church, attorney extraordinaire, a local boy who grew up to become one of Alex Drakos's personal attorneys. That's how good he is."

"Good attorney. Terrible husband?"

"Good attorney. Great husband."

Diallo looked at her. She was tipsy, but she wasn't drunk yet. "If he was so great, why are you divorced?"

"Because I'm a good real estate broker. The best if I may say so myself. That's how I was able to find for you that perfect vacation home you purchased in Pensacola." Then a depressed look came onto her face. "But I was a lousy wife."

Diallo looked at her. "It is understandable," he said.

Faye looked at him. Was that a pickup line? She'd been waiting for his sexy ass to show some signs. "Understandable how?"

"If I may be so bold as to say it? You are so beautiful, Faye Marshall. Perhaps the most beautiful woman I have seen since my arrival in America. You remind me of the women of my native land."

Faye continued to stare at him. Which surprised him. "No blushing?" he asked. "No comment? I would have thought my high-vaulted words would have given you some, how do you say? Pause?"

"Believe it or not," said Faye, "I've been hearing that *you're the most beautiful girl in the world* bullshit ever since I was a child."

"But it is true, no? Did it not help your self-esteem?"

"It destroyed my self-esteem. Destroyed a little of me too." She took another good gulp of her drink.

"How did it destroy you?"

"Because if all you've ever known is men wanting you, then how the hell are you going to want only one man? It's not practical. It's just not. So yes, I lost a very good man because of this great beauty I'm supposed to be." She looked at her gin and tonic. Started moving her glass around, stirring it. "A very good man."

But then she realized what was happening and looked at Diallo. "Slick bastard," she said. "We were talking about you!"

Diallo laughed. "Guilty as charged," he said and lifted his drink as if giving a toast.

"Then answer my question. Have you ever considered settling down with a wife? With kids?"

"Yes, of course." Then something across the room caught his attention. "But the right woman has to come along. She's here."

Faye was confused. "The right woman?"

Diallo smiled. "Mrs. Drakos," he said. "Karena."

"Oh," Faye said and looked oddly at him before looking toward the entrance. And there she was: Kari Grant-Drakos. "There she is."

"Looking as the very definition of elegance and sophistication," said Diallo. "Her dress style is perfection."

"You mean Alex's dress style."

Diallo looked at Faye. "Alex's?"

"Her husband Alex Drakos. He buys all her clothes. He's the one that has her in all of those pearls and diamonds. Kari was never that girl. She used to own a maid service. To this day her main job at The Drakos seems to be supervising the housekeeping staff."

"You are kidding."

"I kid you not. She's the Senior VP or President or whatever big title, but she mainly handles housekeeping. That's Kari."

Diallo nodded. "She's a very good, practical, sensible girl." He looked at Kari as she began making her way toward their table. And he smiled. "I like that."

Faye shook her head. She could never win around Kari. She was considered light years more beautiful than Kari. But men gravitated to Kari as if she was the queen of the world. Faye had her eyes on Alex once. Definitely was interested in seeing where it could go with Diallo. But both men had their sights on Kari. It made no sense to Faye!

"Hey girl," Faye said with a smile as she stood up to greet Kari. Diallo stood up too.

Kari lifted the shades from her eyes and sat them atop her beautiful hair that was in a combination up-do with curls dropped down her back. When she smiled, it seemed, to Diallo, she lit up a room.

Kari was smiling as she hugged her best friend Faye and then she and Diallo hugged.

"Good to see you again, Karena," said Diallo as he held her against him a bit longer than Faye thought was necessary. But Kari didn't seem to complain. But why would she, Faye wondered. Diallo was fine. And not just his body like so many other guys. He had a gorgeous jet-black face to match that jet-black gorgeous body. And his smile, Faye thought, dazzled.

"Sorry I'm so late," Kari said as they all sat down. Kari sat beside Faye in their booth. Which was fine by Diallo. It gave him an unfettered view of her. "I had to wait until Jordan got home to keep the baby."

"I like that your children are so far apart in age," said Diallo. "It means your son will always be a big brother, father-figure to your daughter. And daughters need all the protectors they can get."

"Mamas need that too," said Faye, and she and Kari laughed and leaned against each other.

But as the evening wore on, Faye noticed something startling. Not only was Diallo taking every opportunity to stare at Kari, which wasn't unusual. He was smitten with her, anybody could see that. But Kari was likewise taking peeps at Diallo. That was the unusual part. And when Diallo got a phone call, Faye called Kari on it.

"Excuse me, ladies," Diallo said as he stood up with his ringing phone. "This I must take. Hello," he said as he made his way out of the restaurant for a private conversation.

Faye looked at Kari. "He wants you," she said.

Kari nodded and sipped the drink she had ordered earlier in their meeting. "And I want in too. That's why I'm here. It sounds exactly like what I've been looking for."

"I'm not talking about the investment. I'm

talking about him. Diallo wants you. Sexually and otherwise."

Faye was waiting for Kari to dismiss such talk the way she usually did. But she didn't. She exhaled instead. Which only heightened Faye's suspicion. And she smiled. "I'll be damn. You want him too!"

"I want who?"

"I saw how you were taking peeps at him. And I don't blame you. He's fine as wine. But so is Alex."

"Girl bye. As if I don't have enough on my plate."

"But you were thinking about what life would be with a man like Dee, weren't you, girl? Don't lie. And since you never lie, I know you'll tell me the truth."

But Kari said nothing.

"Well?"

But Kari still said nothing.

Then Faye sighed. "Okay, I'll move on. What all you got on your plate that's got you all in a twist?"

"I'm not in a twist."

"Yes you are. Tell me, girl. You'll feel better if you talk about it."

A look came over Kari. Faye knew that look. "What's going on, Kare? Is it the kids?"

"No. Thank God. No."

55

"Then it must be Alex."

Kari didn't push back on that response.

"What's he done now?"

"He hasn't done anything."

"But?"

"He's got an empire to run. I understand that better than anybody else could. And I have supported him every step of the way."

"Yes, you have. And then some." Then Faye looked at Kari. "But?"

"But I'm tired, Faye. I can't do it anymore. He's never home. And when I say never? He gets home today, and the kids are happy, I'm happy, and then the very next morning we see his suitcases in the foyer and his bodyguard putting them in the limo. And this is all the time."

"That's crazy. Why is he gone so much?"

"The recession, he claims. He's got all of these sectors and these different companies to deal with. But his ass was on the road long before this recession hit."

"But I thought he changed after he almost lost you that time."

"He did. And it lasted a long time too. Real talk. But in the last couple years?" She shook her head. "There's been nothing but go, go, go. Every time I turn around, he has to go. And then the recession hit. And now his company is on the line. *Again*. And it's hyper go, go, go. But even before the hyper, if I'm to be honest, it was getting to be too much."

"Have you talked to him about it?"

"I brought it up. Several times. But like always, Alex isn't hearing me. He insists it's temporary even as I tell him it's not. Him not being neglectful is the temporary shit."

"I'm saying," said Faye. Then she exhaled and looked at Kari. Kari was her girl, she truly was. And she loved Kari. She truly did. But Alex on the market again? Yeah, she would tap the shit out of that. "So," she said. "What do you intend to finally do about it?"

Kari said nothing.

"Inquiring minds want to know," Faye added.

Kari looked at her best friend. "If I leave Alex, you'd be first in line to take my place. Wouldn't you?"

Faye smiled. That was what she loved about her relationship with Kari. They didn't bullshit each other. "I'd be on that white meat like a maggot on raw meat."

Kari smiled and shook her head. "Don't hold back," she joked. "Tell me what you'd really do." And then both of them laughed.

But inwardly, it was no laughing matter for Kari. Because she loved Alex unlike she had ever loved before. Because she knew he was still a good man when good men were harder to find than unicorns. And leaving him was never going to be easy. She was terrified of what leaving Alex would do to her children. But she was equally terrified of what staying with Alex would do to her.

But then Diallo came back, their dinner plates arrived, and it was all laughs and small talk and fun and games all over again.

CHAPTER EIGHT

Eleven that night Alex was back home from Athens and entered the lobby of The Drakos like a man on his last legs. But he still managed to make his way across the lobby and into his hotel's casino. He stood just inside the massive space and watched the crowds gamble and laugh and drink the night away. His kid brother, who was a partner with Alex in the casino and ran that end of his business, saw him and made a quick beeline toward him, his long hair loose and flowing as he walked. *Adonis* was what they nicknamed Oz when they were young men in Greece. And despite Oz's hard living, Alex still could see why.

"Welcome back, brother," Oz said with a grin and with an unlit cigar between his teeth. "You look tired as fuck."

"Anything I need to handle?"

"Absolutely nothing. Like a well-oiled machine, that's how I roll."

Alex looked away from Oz at the boisterous crowds. And this was just the general public area. The VIP gambling lounges were probably even more raucous.

But Oz could see the strain all over his big brother's handsome face. He was stretched too thin. Too many irons in the fire. But there was no telling Alex that. "How did it go? What's the verdict?"

"They're claiming an eighty percent loss in working capital."

Oz was shocked. "Get the fuck out of here! That's bullshit!"

"You know it and I know it."

"How in hell could one sector lose that much revenue? And they're trying to put it all at Galani's feet?"

Alex nodded. "That's what they're trying to do, yes." He looked at Oz. "Any word on her whereabouts?"

"Nothing. Either those fools took her out already, or they have her under the kind of deep cover our people haven't been able to sniff out yet. There's no chatter, no visits to any safe houses, nothing. We've got the entire sector under constant surveillance, but so far we got nothing."

"My money's on they've already harmed her."

But Alex was shaking his head. "They haven't harmed her yet. They may need her to save themselves down the road."

"And you don't think we should go to the

cops?"

"We can't sniff this shit out, but the cops can? And remember we're talking Grecian cops here. Half of those motherfuckers on the take anyway."

Oz nodded. Many of them were on his own payroll. "And not one sector leader will admit shit?"

"Nothing," said Alex. "They're sticking to their lies, and they're sticking together. But I'm not smelling rats for the sweet scent. The men in that room are responsible. It took all I had not to waste every one of those bastards."

"Who's the ringleader? Dave Pantanzis?"

"Yep."

"Ungrateful asshole! We've known him since we were all in Pop's syndicate together. You taught him everything he knows. You gave him the chance to go legit and run the day-to-day in your Greek sector, and it was working like a charm. But if what we suspect is true, it'll be a major betrayal, Alexio. And for him to even think about harming Galani after all she's done for him, too, and when he knows what she means to you?"

Alex exhaled and placed his hands in his pockets. "They don't give a shit about that anymore. Which is fine. But they're going to restore my money and my CEO, and they've got thirty days to do so."

"You put that ultimatum on the table?"

"Along with my Glock," said Alex. "Yes."

Oz grinned. "You left the gangster world far behind you my ass."

Alex smiled a weak smile too.

But then Oz turned serious again. "Stateside still looking anemic?"

Alex nodded. "My team and I have been noticing some volatility there, yes. The markets are waiting to see what will happen with this merger, but if it falls through we could be right back in danger zone again."

"Damn," said Oz. "It's this fucking recession. Everybody's hurting. Especially the banking sector. Thank goodness we aren't them."

"But we are them if lending dries up," Alex reminded his brother. "They fail and we won't be far behind."

Oz nodded. "High finance is a rollercoaster ride."

"Every day God send," said Alex. Then he wiped the palm of his hand across his face. Sometimes he wondered how he ever managed to put one foot in front of the other one given all of the crises he had to deal with. "I'm dead on my feet," he said. "I'm going to bed."

"So soon? The night is still so young!"

"Only to lazy motherfuckers like you," said Alex.

Oz laughed. "Sweet dreams, my brother."

Alex threw up his hand in a wave goodbye as he made his way out of the casino, across the lobby, and onto his private elevator that took him up to the penthouse where he and his family resided.

When he entered the penthouse, he walked around the long hall of the foyer and into his living room. Jordan was laying on the couch texting on his phone and twisting one of his hair twists around his finger, while his baby girl Angela was asleep at the other end, at Jordan's feet.

Alex leaned against the jamb of the archway and gazed at his children. Jordan was his wife's biological son, a beautiful African-American young man with the brains to match his beauty. The only thing he was terrible at were sports. But he did his best there too. Alex loved him so much that he adopted him and made him his own. One of the happiest days of his life. He could not have been prouder of that young man.

And Angela. His angel. He smiled as he watched her sleep. She was just a little fireball of a princess in waiting. Jordan was going to give him nothing but joy. He could feel it in his bones. But if he and Kari weren't ever so careful with Angela, on the other hand, they were going to have their hands full.

He pushed away from the jamb and made his way to the sofa. It was only then did Jordan tear his eyes away from his phone to realize his father was home. "Oh hey Dad," he said, and promptly returned his attention back to his phone. He refused to get all excited when his father came back into town now. His leaving was happening too regular. It had gone on too long.

"Where's Mom?" Alex asked. He had expected to see Kari roaming around downstairs somewhere.

But all Jordan did was hunch his shoulders.

"What does that mean, Jordan? Put that damn phone down and talk to me."

Jordan, who loved Alex but feared him too, looked away from his phone and up at his father. He was a great dad, but Jordan also knew that Alex would knock him through a wall if he even thought about disobeying him. "She was leaving when I got home. Told me to babysit and that she'd be back."

"You didn't ask her where she was

going?"

"I asked. All she said was that she was going to dinner."

"To dinner?"

"That's what she said."

"Did she say with whom?"

"No, sir."

"And you didn't ask?"

Jordan didn't like that he seemed to be blaming him. "No, sir."

"Why not?"

Jordan frowned. "Why I needed to ask? She said she was going to dinner. You should have been here then you'd know all those other questions."

Alex was staring at Jordan. He was pissed with him, too, for not being home enough. But that didn't give him a license to be disrespectful. "Watch your tone, young man," he said.

Jordan realized he had crossed a line. Despite the absences, Alex was still Jordan's hero. "Yes, sir."

"What time did you get home?"

"Six-ish. Maybe seven."

Now it was almost eleven. Which would make a long-ass dinner. Alex let out a sigh of frustration and picked up his baby girl. "She been sleeping long?"

"Not long, no."

"What's not long, Jordan?"

"An hour. Maybe two."

Alex wanted to roll his eyes. These young people and their phones! They didn't pay attention to shit. But he, instead, gave Jordan a hug. Jordan, who loved his father's affection, gave him a hug too.

"Don't stay up too late," he said as he began carrying Angela away. "It's still a school night."

Did he forget Jordan was in college now? But Jordan didn't argue with him. "Yes, sir," he said. And returned to his phone.

And Alex, with his baby girl, made his way upstairs to his bedroom, laid prone on the bed and laid a still-sleeping Angela beside him, and phoned his wife.

But the call went to Voice Mail. Which meant she had her phone turned off.

Alex knew he was always admonishing her about trusting him, and he knew he had to do the same with her. Which was easy. He did trust his wife. But that wasn't his main concern. Her safety always was his main concern. And for that reason he phoned the chief of her security detail.

"She's alright, sir," the detail chief said. "She's having dinner at Piper's with Mrs.

Marshall, and a gentleman."

"Is that gentleman Benny Church?" Alex asked.

"It's not Mrs. Marshall's ex-husband, no sir. We don't know the gentleman, except to say that she's had dinner with him several other times over the last few months."

Alex frowned. "The last few months?"

"Yes, sir."

"Faye included every time?"

"Mrs. Marshall was there the first time we saw him, yes sir. But tonight was only the second time we've seen Mrs. Marshall have dinner with Mrs. Drakos and the gentleman."

"Do you have a photo of the gentleman?"

"Yes, sir."

"Send it to me," Alex ordered, and ended the call.

Within seconds the photo arrived. And just as he feared the smiling face of the man staring back at him was a sight to behold. Much younger than Alex, more around Kari's age, he was a total hunk of a black man with an undeniable strong look. Alex's first instinct was to hop into his car and get to that restaurant. But that wasn't his style. He had to trust his wife. And her detail chief confirmed she was safe. He had no excuse to go over there.

But the fact that Kari had been having

dinner with this great hunk of male for months was a major revelation. But it wasn't as if Alex had been around to notice. He'd been putting out fire after fire in his conglomerate of businesses ever since an unforeseen recession rocked the country once again. But now there just might be a fire in his own home and he knew nothing about it?

He closed his eyes and leaned his head back. All he needed, he thought.

CHAPTER NINE

Around three in the early morning hours, Kari woke up in bed with Alex deep inside of her. She loved the feeling of his deepest penetration and couldn't stifle a groan as soon as she woke up and felt it. She was on top of Alex. They were both naked in bed. And he was moving inside of her with the expertise of a master of his craft.

"*Aah,*" she was saying repeatedly as he did her, and he was moaning and groaning sounds of satisfaction too.

He had been in Europe for nearly a week and a half straight and she had no idea he was returning last night. Or she would have been home. Or she would have told Diallo no, she couldn't make it, and waited at home for her husband. He was fast asleep when she got home. She put the baby in her own bed and went to bed too.

But some time, as late night turned into early morning, his ass woke up.

But a part of Kari was pissed with Alex anyway. Gone a week-and-a-half and not one phone call from him? She knew he was busy. Hell, she was busy trying to run that big-ass hotel of his too! But she tried to phone him all the time. Left text messages too. But he never bothered to text or phone her back.

When he was home, he was great. But he was still leaving far too much.

But she knew he knew that his dick was her pleasure center. That his dick cured all that ailed her in that moment. And he was putting it on her good.

And when Kari began to orgasm, she could hardly bear the force of her cum. She was pulsating so hard that she felt as if she was levitating and Alex was arched up to make certain that dick kept pounding her. And she loved every pound. She came furiously.

Alex didn't cum by design. As his eyes were watching Kari like laser beams as she came, he refused to let his pleasure interrupt what he felt he needed to do. He was branding her again. There could be no doubt about that. He wanted her whipped again. He wanted her to need him again. He wanted to make it clear to her that no man could take his place inside of her and they'd better not try. He wanted to make it crystal clear that he wished a motherfucker would!

But when it required more willpower than Alex was able to muster, he gave up the fight and wrapped Kari into his arms and came all over the inside of her. It was as if a dam broke he poured so hard into her.

Kari felt it too. He knew Alex was marking his territory just from the sheer intensity of his lovemaking. He was laying down pipes and he wasn't trying to hide it either. And Kari had a good idea why. His spies masquerading as her hidden security detail, had undoubtedly told him that she had yet another dinner date with Diallo.

But so what? His ass was always around the world having dinner dates with great looking ladies all the time, and what was she supposed to do about that? Sit around and take it? At least she and Diallo were talking business. Were trying to go into business together. She had no idea what Alex and his ladies were "discussing."

But his actions were speaking louder than any words he could have said. He was making it clear that he was her man. But what Alex never seemed to get wasn't that he was her man. She knew who he was. But the fact that he had to make it clear was the issue. He never wanted to discuss the issue.

And sure enough, after their lovemaking, Alex never once mentioned who the guy was she had been having dinner with, or why. He didn't ask her anything. Not about her day. Not about her life. It was as if he didn't want to poke the bear. Just pretend it didn't need poking.

They fell asleep in each other's arms.

And when she woke up, later that morning, Alex, *being Alex*, had already gone to work.

CHAPTER TEN

ONE WEEK LATER

"A mall, Kari?" Oz Drakos looked over at his sister-in-law with a look of confusion on his face. She was behind the wheel of her Bentley, wearing sunglasses, her long hair draped down her back in waves of curls, her gorgeous dark face looking puzzled too. "He asked you to meet him at a mall?"

Kari thought it was an odd location, too, when Diallo asked her to meet him in Pensacola at the largest mall in the region, but she wasn't trying to explain a damn thing to Oz. It wasn't his business. "I don't see why you need to be here anyway."

"I'm here because our boss, my beloved big brother and your beloved big husband, ordered me, before he left town, to blanket you. I didn't ask questions. I just do what I'm told."

"And what if I told your ass to leave? What then?"

"Then I'll respect your wishes and leave. But I'll still blanket you."

Kari looked at him. "That don't make no kind of sense."

"It makes sense to me! I'm scared of you, I'll freely admit that. I am one alpha male who is afraid of his small but mighty sister-in-law. Because your temper, once unleashed, is something to talk about. I'm scared of you, yes, I am. But I'm terrified of my brother. You don't just talk about his temper. You feel it. Fist after motherfucking fist. His temper is legendary!"

Kari couldn't help but laugh. Oz was always good for a laugh. "Boy bye," she said.

Oz grinned that infectious grin and snatched his own long hair back. "But for real, Kare, what's with the mall? Who, in this day and age, has a business meeting at a mall?"

"Diallo, that's who."

"Dallo? What kind of name is that anyway?"

"It's Diallo. "Dee-Al-low. Diallo. It's an African name. He's African."

Oz looked at Kari. "You mean African as in African-American? Or African as in real African?"

Kari shook her head. "Gloria ain't teaching your ass nothing about our culture, is she?"

But Oz wasn't playing this time. "Kari, I'm serious."

Kari looked at him again. "Why you so serious about what I'm doing? So you can report back to your brother? He's African, okay? He's from Nigeria."

"If you tell me he's a Nigerian prince who need you to send him a money order, we getting up out of here right now!"

Kari laughed again and shook her head. "He's nobody's prince. Trust and believe."

Now Oz was seriously worried. "What's that supposed to mean?"

"He's a businessman, Oz. That's all you need to know."

That was what she thought, but Oz wasn't thinking like that. Whenever Alex was out of town, he was daddy. He was in charge of the family. Even though he and Kari were very close in age, and both were younger than Alex, that didn't matter to Oz. "Diallo what? What's his last name?"

"Koffi."

"I thought that was a first name, like Kofi Anan from the UN."

"He has two F's in his name. Kofi Annan has one."

Oz pulled out his phone and began Googling that name. When Kari saw it, she ignored it. She was used to Oz and Alex's overbearingness. She didn't like it one bit. And their asses wouldn't like it at all if she flipped the script on them. But she and Gloria both were used to the hypocrisy of those Drakos brothers.

Oz was amazed at the number of articles that popped up when he googled that name. A book of articles popped up, in fact, and they were all business-related. And Kari was right. He was definitely no prince. He was Fortune 500 big. Which meant he was a bad boy just like the rest of the big boys. You didn't get to be big, in Oz's world, without being ruthless.

But when Oz saw Diallo's face, his heart dropped. To call Diallo Koffi good looking would be the understatement of the century. He was fantastic looking with that dark chocolate flawless skin, those big, gorgeous deep brown eyes, and a bright white smile that would clearly light up the universe. And this was the man Kari was looking to go into business with? This undoubtedly well-hung hunk? Oz was beginning to think his brother's marriage might just be in more trouble than it already appeared to be. But when he read the next bit of information about him, Oz didn't think it anymore. He knew it. This guy wasn't just some random, he was on Alex's level. He could very well become Alex's competition.

Oz looked at Kari. "And he's a billionaire too?"

"*Too*? What do you mean by *too*?"

"Come on, Kare. This is Oz you're talking

to. I'm straight as straight can get, everybody knows that. But a guy who looks this good, even I would be smitten. I'll meet his ass at the mall! What gives?"

Kari exhaled and leaned back against the headrest. "He's in the country looking to form a conglomerate and go into business with his people."

"*His* people?"

"African-Americans. Black people. He wants an all-minority-owned Fortune 500 company. And I want to be a part of that too."

"Since when?"

"I've always wanted that."

"And of all the people he could have invited to the table, he invites you, a woman married to a white man?"

"I invited myself actually."

Oz found that an odd thing to say. "How could you invite yourself?"

"Faye was invited to the table until she found out the digits that would be involved. So I asked her to put him in touch with me."

"What kind of digits?"

"Major. Fifty million plus to get in the conversation."

"Shit!" said Oz. "Get the fuck out of here! Fifty million dollars? For what percentage?"

"A very small percentage. We'll talking

Fortune 500, Oz. It's not going to be nickels and dimes. And Diallo will own the lion's share. Something like over ninety percent. But he feels guilty and really wants to do this for his people."

"He's not feeling *that* guilty if he's getting ninety percent." But then Oz thought about what she said. "He's feels guilty about what?"

"Slavery. The participation of some Africans in rounding up our people to be transported. And the fact that his continent didn't try to get us back."

This guy was just odd, Oz thought. "His country wouldn't have been able to compete against the west and their firepower."

"You know that, and I know that. But that's how he feels. He wants to give back, he says. And thus this meeting."

It sounded like bullshit to Oz, but maybe it wasn't. And the fact that Faye had been in the picture concerned him too. Faye Marshall was Kari's best friend, and good peeps all around. But she loved herself some good-looking men, that was why her ass couldn't keep a great guy like Benny. But talk about a legend. Faye and her various trysts were legendary in Apple Valley.

"Where's Gloria?" asked Kari. Gloria, who, like Kari, was African-American too, was Oz's wife.

When Oz didn't respond, Kari looked at him. "You was all mouth when it was my business. Where's Glo, Oz? She might want to join our investment group."

"I doubt that."

"Where is she?"

He didn't immediately respond, but eventually he did. "Philly."

"Again? She and the baby?"

"Yep."

Kari knew what that meant. "What your ass did this time?"

"My ass didn't do shit," said Oz, looking at his sister-in-law. "Why you and Alex always blaming me? Why does it always have to be my fault?"

"Because it always is," said Kari, not backing down.

Oz exhaled. Kari knew then it was some shit he did. "I was talking to some ladies in the casino and she showed up. She got into it with one of the ladies and because I thought it was stupid, because it was, she and I got into it. And she bounced like she always does. But all of that running home to daddy shit is getting old."

"I agree. But you knew that child was like that when you married her, Oz. She's got daddy issues as big as a river, even I could have told you that. That's why she married your

79

domineering ass. That's why she married somebody just like her daddy. Just like Mick."

Oz frowned. "Me? Like hell! I'm nothing like that mean motherfucker. Don't even try that, Kare."

Then the conversation ended. Because Oz was talkative as he could be, but was quiet as a mouse when it came to his shit. So it shut down. Until Oz changed the subject back to the subject at hand. "Are you sure this guy is who he claims to be?"

"Yes, Odysseus. He's a bona fide billionaire who is not pretentious or showy in any way. He's just a man who does his work and get it done. I had three different teams check him out on deep, deep background before I agreed to even meet with him the first time."

Oz looked at her. "You've met with him before?"

"Yes! I've known him for months. We've had about ten or even a dozen meetings since Faye hooked me up with him."

This surprised Oz. But he also knew Alex had to have been in town every time she held those meetings. Alex gave her much more liberty when he was in town. Unless. . . "So Alex knows about him?"

Kari hesitated, which told Oz all he needed to know. "This has nothing to do with

Alex. This investment, should I decide to make it, is my thing. My deal."

"But a dozen meetings, Kare, and Alex doesn't know about any of them?" Oz had a voice dripping with skepticism.

"So what if I met with him a dozen times? Alex don't be inviting my ass to any of his business meetings. Why should I invite him to mine when it has nothing to do with him?"

But that fifty mill was going to have a lot to do with Alex, since it was going to be Alex's money she was shelling out. But that was beside the point to Oz. The fact that she mentioned that it had nothing to do with Alex twice already let Oz know it had everything to do with Alex. Because he knew the signs. Married lady trying to get her independence, and stake her own claim, before she dropped the divorce bomb and changed the game.

Not that Oz blamed her. Alex could sometimes be a very attentive husband and father. The best in fact. But sometimes, maybe most times, he could be off the reservation doing his own thing. Because that was how the Drakos men rolled. They did their own thing. That was how Oz rolled too. And that was why Gloria and his little girl were in Philly, not Florida with him, at that very moment.

But if it truly wasn't about Alex, but about

another man? That would be another story entirely. Because Oz knew his brother. And he knew if any man even tried to look at Kari too hard, world war three would break out in that bitch.

"Here he is," said Kari.

Oz looked at her. "Here's who?" *The other man*? he almost slipped and asked.

"Diallo." Kari watched as a Ford Taurus pulled up beside them.

Oz looked at that car and shook his head. "A billionaire in a Ford?" Then he looked at Kari. "Seriously?"

"It's a rental while he's in Florida. I told you he's not flashy in any way, shape, or form. I told you there's not a pretentious bone in his body."

How would she know, after only ten meetings, Oz wanted to say. But he looked at that car again, instead, and the thought of it made him smile. "I like him. No bodyguards. No entourage." He looked at Kari, nodding and grinning. "I like him already."

Kari smiled, shook her head at her eccentric brother-in-law, and then she and Oz got out of her Bentley and walked around to the front of the car.

Diallo Koffi may have been driving an unpretentious car, but when he got out of that car, Oz could see that his dress style was another matter. His well-crafted Italian suit fit him like a second skin as he walked over to the twosome. Oz was tall, and Diallo matched his height. Oz also noticed that he had an athletic build that could rival his own and Alex's physiques. He was the real deal.

"Karena," Diallo said happily in his clear English-African accented diction, as he moved past Oz and gave Kari a giant bear hug.

"Hello, Dee," Kari said happily, too, as they hugged.

"It's so good to see you again," Diallo said. Their hug, in Oz's estimation, was a bit longer that was appropriate, and too tight on Diallo's end, but he knew he was biased.

Kari would have agreed with Oz that the embrace was a bit much, but she was always so happy to see Diallo's smiling face. He seemed so genuine to her. And he was truthful too. He told everybody he was no angel. But Kari never trusted perfect guys anyway. She always steered toward the bad boy types. And his arms around her always felt so good, but so strange too. Because before Diallo, nobody made her feel so protected in their arms except for Alex.

When they stopped embracing, she introduced him to Oz. "This is my brother-in-law Odysseus Drakos. But everybody calls him Oz."

"Oz, oh yes," said Diallo as he extended his hand. "Karena has mentioned you before. It is with pleasure that I meet you now."

"Nice to meet you too," said Oz, putting on his best smile as they shook hands. He had strong anti-feelings about the guy, but he didn't want to antagonize him yet. He needed to know what he was truly about first.

But as they made their way into the mall, and Diallo placed his hand on Kari's back to let her go in ahead of him, as if she was *his* woman, Oz's bad feeling continued. But he kept his feelings to himself.

CHAPTER ELEVEN

"I hope he doesn't shoot the messenger."

Ezekiel, Alex's chief negotiator, along with Cal, his assistant, looked at Paige, Alex's chief accountant. They were all waiting in the hotel lobby of The Carson-Benning hotel in Manhattan. "You think you're going to tell him something he doesn't already know about his own conglomerate? The markets have already opened. You don't think he saw those numbers? We're sinking faster than the Titanic. Losing more shares today than we did yesterday, which means our P.R. people can't claim a one-off anymore. Even the Street is nervous. But you don't think Boss is? "

"I know he is," Paige responded. "But I don't think he truly understands the gravity here, Zeke. We're talking an eighty-billion-dollar corporation that's now valued south of seventy-one billion. That's a nine-billion-dollar devaluation already."

Ezekiel frowned. "What's driving this shit? What's happening?"

"The recession and now this merger," said Paige. "That's what's driving it. The experts don't think it's going to happen.

Moody's and the S & P are giving it a downgrade. If we don't merge, we're in danger zone."

Ezekiel shook his head. "We just pulled back from the brink. Now we're back on the brink again?"

"Welcome to the world of high finance," said Paige. "Brinks never end. Until they do and you end up in the corporate graveyard. Just ask Lehman Brothers. They'll tell you. But I'm certain Mr. Drakos will put his own personal fortune on the line before he lets that happen."

Ezekiel and Cal looked at each other. "Compared to us, she's a rookie," said Cal. "Cut her some slack. She'll learn."

"She'd better, or Boss will teach her. And he's no fucking teacher."

Ezekiel and Cal laughed, and even Paige joined in too.

But it was no laughing matter when the elevator opened and the boss stepped off. All three stood up when Alex entered the lobby, flanked by his longtime bodyguard, and made his way toward the exit.

"Hello, sir," said Ezekiel, the most senior of the three aides. He hurried to keep up with the boss's long strides. But Alex ignored him.

"Hello, sir," said Cal, hurrying too, with Alex ignoring him as well.

Paige was always impressed with Alex's dress style as he moved to walk by her, and he didn't disappoint: in a radiant periwinkle blue, he was sporting Armani head to toe, if she had to venture a guess. And the way his unbuttoned suitcoat flowed effortlessly when he walked, compared to Zeke and Cal's suitcoats that seemed to fly around their bodies uncontrollably, impressed her too. He was just a gorgeous, sexy, man's man. She'd give up a limb to be his woman. "Good morning, sir," she said with a grand smile as he walked by her.

But Alex didn't acknowledge her either. He didn't have a word to say to any of them until he got into his limousine, with his bodyguard getting on the front seat, and his three aides getting in on the opposite seat directly in front of Alex's lone seat. It had been a long week in New York, with longwinded meetings with several partners who were scared shitless by the downturn. And now this merger had taken on epic proportions he never wanted it to take on. But the markets got ahead of him. And he wasn't trying to be polite to his employees and he didn't mince words. "I don't want the bullshit," said Alex. "I want the bottom line as you see it today."

"We're bleeding massively," said Paige. "There's no other way to put it. After the markets opened, we've been on the phones with Corporate all morning and everybody reached the same conclusion. If we don't get this deal done, and done today, we just may bleed out."

"As soon as things are looking up again," said Ezekiel, "another recession slaps us in the face. Now we're back on our heels again. Now we've got to have another deal again. It's been like a fucking rollercoaster ride."

"It's not just us," Paige pointed out, and Alex looked at her. "Everybody's bleeding."

"But they aren't a *got*damn gorilla like we are," said Ezekiel. "We fail, we take damn near a third of the market with us."

"My point is," said Paige, "we're in a hole. But instead of wallowing in it, we need solutions. Because Zeke is right. The numbers are the numbers. And they are anemic at best. But there are some options," she said as she pulled out a folder and reached it over to Alex, which shocked her superiors Ezekiel and Cal. But Alex didn't reach for it anyway.

"There are options," said Ezekiel, pulling Paige's now-dangling folder back toward Paige, "but none of them are viable. We've discussed this already," he said, glancing over at Paige. Then he looked at Alex. "This merger is not a debatable issue anymore, Boss. We have got to agree to whatever terms end up on the table."

"No matter what," added Cal.

"We can't leave New York without a deal," said Ezekiel. "That's the real bottom line."

Alex looked at Zeke. He and Zeke went back nearly a decade. He trusted his judgment. "Who am I meeting with? The CEO or Bev?"

"Beverly, unfortunately, sir. And you know she'll come out swinging, especially given our plummet this morning after the opening bell. She always comes out swinging."

Alex looked out of the window as the limo began pulling off, and he couldn't suppress a harsh exhale. "All I need," he said.

CHAPTER TWELVE

They made their way into the food court, which was the heart of the mall, and met up with another black man who was waiting for them. "Hey, Rho," Kari said and embraced him too. But this time with a lot less vigor than she embraced Diallo. "This is Rhodale Scotts, my numbers man," said Kari to Diallo. "But we call him Rho. Rho, meet Diallo Koffi."

After Rho and Koffi shook hands and exchanged pleasantries, Kari introduced Rho to Oz. "And this is my brother-in-law Odysseus Drakos."

"But everybody calls me Oz," Oz said as he and Rho shook hands. He didn't know Kari had a numbers man.

"Very nice to meet you," Rho said.

"You're Kari's accountant?" Oz asked.

"I am."

Oz nodded his head, but glanced at Kari. Since when did she need her own personal accountant when Alex had a team of accountants working for him? Oz realized that this wasn't some passing fancy for Kari. She was serious about this shit.

And as they all stood there talking about

Florida heat and other bullshit topics as if they were there to just hang out, Oz's feelings toward Diallo began to crystallize. Because her recognized that kind of man. Oz came from a family of gangsters. His old man, when he was still alive, ran the most infamous crime syndicate in all of Greece once upon a time. Even his big brother Alex was the enforcer for that organization before he left and never looked back. And although not common knowledge, Oz himself was still steeped in that gangster world. He tried to get out like his brother did, but Oz had been in far too long for any thoughts of getting out. He was *gangsterized*. There was no getting out.

Diallo, in Oz's estimation, was *gangsterized* too. Oz could see it written all over him. He wanted to "give back" to his people about as much as a mountain lion swallowing his prey wanted to give it back. Oz was keeping his eyes on him.

But out of the corner of his eyes, as Kari, Diallo, and Rho kept going on about little of nothing, Oz saw a woman staring at him. A gorgeous blonde. When he turned and looked at her, he smiled.

"I thought that was you!" she said to him. "Hello, Oz."

"Jill?" Oz recognized her too. He hadn't

seen her in years. They used to be fuck partners, but little more than that. But that was a major problem in his world. He had had so many such partners before he married Gloria, that everywhere he turned he was running into one. But he also remembered that Jill made for good conversation too. And since she was not that far away from where Kari was standing, and Kari and her group were boring the hell out of him, he went over to Jill, gave her a hug, and they began conversing about little of nothing too.

But as soon as Oz left the group, Diallo got down to business. "I did not want to discuss the specifics in front on anybody but the three of us. This is a need-to-know conversation."

"Understood," said Rho.

But Kari found it odd. "What do you think Oz was going to do? Take the idea from underneath you? He wouldn't do that."

"I confess I do not know him the way you do, Karena. I have to go by my instincts in these matters. I do apologize."

"No worries," said Rho, who seemed in total agreement with Diallo's caution. "You were saying?"

"The reason I asked you to come, Kari, and to bring your accountant, is so that I could introduce you two to our very first investment."

Kari and Rho waited for Diallo to continue. When Diallo didn't continue, Kari asked him outright. "Well? What's going to be our very first investment?"

Diallo smiled. "You're standing in it."

Rho looked at Kari. Kari was looking around. "What? This food court?"

Diallo smiled again. "No, Karena, not the food court. This mall. This entire mall."

Kari and Rho both were shocked. "It's for sale?"

"Yes. But it's a pocket listing. Only a few eyes have been accorded the opportunity to purchase it at this point. I'm one of those few eyes. And guess what? Should we purchase it, all of the businesses must apply for new leases with us. Which means, we can determine what stores will be in this mall, and what stores will be axed."

"Underperforming stores will be axed," said Kari.

Diallo nodded. "Correct. And they will be replaced with black-owned businesses. I want at least fifty percent of all businesses in this mall to be black-owned. Not minority owned. That's how they can circumvent giving us our fair share. I mean black owned."

Kari nodded. "Wow. That'll be a first."

"Yes, it will, given the scope and sheer

size of this mall. It will open a lot of doors for lots of black companies that never stood a chance. I'm quite excited about it actually."

Kari smiled. "So am I," she admitted. "But the fact that it's for sale worries me."

"Yes, me too," said Rho. "What is the financial health of this place?"

"It's good. Not great, granted. But good," said Diallo. "It could use," he started saying when a sudden loud pop sound was heard. Before they could even look around to see what it was, a volley of pop sounds began to be heard and Oz knew just as Diallo apparently knew that they weren't pop sounds at all. Shots were being fired! Loud, rapid, machine gun-style rounds of shots.

Oz, forgetting his old fuck partner, tried to rush over to shield Kari, but Diallo had already knocked Kari down himself and fallen on top of her, shielding her body with his own as he began moving her behind a display case in the middle of the food court.

Oz hurried behind them, pulling out his gun as Diallo and Kari were pulling out their weapons too, and all three began firing back on what they saw was a lone gunman near the back of the massive food court. Oz knew he'd hit the gunman at least twice. But the gunman was wearing such well-fortified, high-tech body armor that covered every single inch of his body, including his head. The only part of his body not fully covered was the upper half of his face, near his eyes, which meant none of their bullets could penetrate him.

That was why Diallo got up and began running toward the gunman, shooting as he ran, and Oz and Kari, shocked that he had gotten up, began shooting to give him some cover. They understood why Diallo was rushing the gunman. They all realized they needed to give that gunman a facial if they were going to take him out. His face was the only non-protected part of his body. They had to hit him in the face.

And Diallo did just that. He stopped where he stood, called out the gunman, and as soon as the gunman turned his way, he fired on him before the gunman could fire back, hitting him between the eyes. It was a gangster shot, Oz thought, because it was a perfect bullseye. The gunman fell backwards, and his assault-style rifle fell sideways.

Oz looked at Kari. Kari nodded anxiously. "I'm good," she said. "You?"

"I'm good," said Oz as he got up and helped Kari up.

But as they hurried to go to where Diallo and the gunman were, they realized many had been hit around them. Including Rhodale Scotts and Oz's friend Jill.

"Rho!" Kari cried as she hurried over to Rho and fell on her knees. And Oz, shocked too, hurried over to Jill. Although Rhodale had a pulse still, Jill had none. Oz was beside himself. All he had to do was knock her down. All he had to do was make one extra movement before rushing to aid Kari. But when he heard that gunfire, he could think of nobody else but Kari. And what his brother would have done to him had Kari been hit. What he would have done to himself had Kari been hit. He didn't give Jill a second thought.

Diallo hurried over to Rho too. "He's alive," said Kari, "but he needs help fast."

"Ambulances are on the way," said a man who wore the uniform of one of the managers in the food court. "Tell him to hold on," he added, and hurried to check on the others who had fallen.

But as Diallo helped Kari up from her knees, Kari was looking at Diallo. "You saved my life," she said to him. Oz heard her, and looked over too. "I was standing right beside Rho," she added. "If you wouldn't have knocked me down, that could have been me."

Oz knew it too. He stared at Diallo. It was a great thing that he was there and that his first instinct was to save Kari. But the fact that

that was his first instinct wasn't great. The fact that saving Kari meant more to him than saving himself spoke loudly to Oz. A dozen meetings. Months getting to know him. A great looking, seemingly nice guy. It spoke volumes to Oz.

But when Diallo looked at Kari as if he, too, realized what a close call it had been, and that look in his eyes was that same look he'd seen Alex give to Kari, that look of love that nobody could deny, Oz's heart began to pound even more than it was already pounding. And when Kari was staring at Diallo, as if they'd just had a very special moment together, and when Diallo pulled her into his arms in another one of their too-close, too-tight bearhugs, Oz's heart skipped a beat.

Trouble had come to town in the form of this life-saving, sexy African. And none of their lives, somehow Oz knew instinctively, would ever be the same again.

CHAPTER THIRTEEN

The limousine stopped in front of the Norgate Corporate office building in the flatiron district of southern Manhattan and Tad Vrekek, the CEO, opened Alex's door and extended his hand.

"Welcome to Norgate, Mr. Drakos," said Tad as the two men shook hands. "It's been a long time."

Alex's team, and his bodyguard, also got out of the limo. They followed the boss and CEO into the building.

But once they made it up to the top floor, and stepped off of the elevator, only Alex was allowed to go into the office of the Chairman. But that was no surprise to any of them. They knew that was how Bev Norgate rolled. They waited with bated breath.

But Alex wasn't holding his breath. He knew Bev too well. And sure enough, when he entered her lair, he had to call her name twice and go around the corner of her massive office to her "resting" room. A room with a bed. A bed she was lying upon, totally naked. But Alex expected nothing less.

"Still thirsty I see," he said to her with a

smile, causing her to laugh out loud.

"Thirsty, yes," she said as he sat down in a chair in the room. "But only for you, sweetheart," she added. Her accent was heavy, kind of Zza-Zza Gabor-ish in Alex's estimation. "But I still look fantastic, do I not?"

"You look very nice." He was a man, not a stone. He was getting a hard-on. "But I'm not here for your looks."

"No, you are here for my money." She smiled. "Am I wrong?"

Alex liked the honesty of their relationship. "No. You're not wrong."

"You are far richer than I shall ever be, but you need my money. So ironic. Why?"

"If Norgate merges into my North American conglomerate," said Alex, "we will be the force to be reckoned with."

"And if I do not merge into The Drakos Conglomerate, what then? Drakos will die, no? I will not. I am not so big that I will fail. But Drakos will fail. And thus, the great man has personally paid me a visit."

Alex studied Beverly Norgate. Same great body. And beautiful still. They used to hang out back in the day all the time, but only to an end: he was using her to get next to her father, who was the king of the mountain back then. She was using him strictly for sex. It was a mutual respect built on honesty above all. And still was.

"What's your bottom line, Bev?" he asked her.

"Fuck me the way you used to do it, because no man has topped it yet, and the deal is done. Refuse me this one great pleasure, and no deal. That's the bottom line." She said this and looked at Alex as if it wasn't preposterous what she had just proposed. He was staring at her.

Then the door to her office opened, and she went apoplectic. "No one comes into my office without my strict permission!" she screamed.

"Alex, it's an emergency!" It was Ezekiel's voice. He dared not go beyond the entrance door.

But Alex knew Zeke would not bother him unless it was beyond important. He quickly got up and walked back around and into the main office. When he saw Ezekiel's face, he knew it was bad. "What is it?"

"It's your wife."

Alex's heart dropped. "What about my wife?"

"There was a mass shooting at the mall in Pensacola, sir. And she was there."

Alex thought it was a joke, but knew it

wasn't. Zeke didn't have that kind of liberty with him. "She was hit?"

"No, sir. She was not. But it apparently was very close."

Alex felt the sting of what that meant.

"Oz felt you should know."

"Absolutely!" said Alex. And he began hurrying for the exit.

"But sir," said Ezekiel, and Alex turned to him. "You can't leave yet. If we don't do this deal today, we'll in trouble."

"And my wife isn't?" said a now angry Alex. He left without looking back.

"Is that you, Zeke?" Bev called out.

CHAPTER FOURTEEN

Kari, Oz, and Diallo watched as the paramedics piled Rhodale Scotts into the ambulance outside of the mall and the ambulance took off. Other ambulances and police cars were everywhere. People were being triaged, treated, and some were even being airlifted to nearby hospitals. Many people were hit. Some, like Oz's friend Jill, died. And Kari, though trying her best to put on a brave face, was shaken. And Oz and Diallo were both trying with all they had to get her to go to the hospital for evaluation.

"I don't need an evaluation," Kari said as she began heading for her Bentley. The Police had already questioned all of them and let them go.

But Diallo wouldn't let it go. "I will feel better, Karena, if you are evaluated."

"I don't care how you'll feel," Kari shot back as they walked, "but I don't like hospitals and I'm not going to one."

"No hospital," said Diallo. "I am not speaking of a hospital. I wish that you would allow my medical team to evaluate you. You've met my doctors before. They are the best of the best. Please, Karena."

What doctors Kari met, Oz wondered as Kari stopped walking and looked at Diallo. The fact that she was even considering something so absurd confounded Oz.

"They have the equipment to run a few tests just to make sure there is no internal damage. We do not want you to go home later and it is too late."

Kari exhaled. The sincere look of concern on Dee's face impressed her. And his rationale made sense too. "Okay," she said. "But only a few tests."

Diallo smiled. "Very well."

"And another thing," said Kari. "We take my car."

Diallo laughed. "No worries. I will have my man pick up mine later. Let me make the arrangements." Diallo pulled out his phone as he walked further away.

Kari began heading to her Bentley again, but Oz grabbed her arm and pulled her back. "Kare, wait."

Kari turned and looked at him.

"Where is this clinic he's taking you to?"

"It's not a clinic. It's a mansion he owns here in Pensacola that he stays in whenever he's in Florida. It has a medical ward inside."

"A medical ward inside his house? Are

you saying you've been there before?"

Kari would rather not go there with Oz. "Yes," she said, and headed for her car.

Oz stood there looking at her as if he was seeing her for the first time. He always was certain it was going to be Alex that would break up their happy home. Alex was the odds-on favorite hands down. But now Kari was in the game? Angelic Karena? For perhaps the first time in his life, Oz was speechless.

CHAPTER FIFTEEN

The plane landed at the airfield just as Oz and Jordan drove up in Kari's Bentley. They stepped out as Alex hurried down the air steps and across the tarmac. Jordan was glad to see his father, but he knew his mood swings. And when he was worried about Jordan's mother, his mood was never good. Jordan knew he had to tread carefully.

But as soon as his father stepped off of that plane and began heading their way, Jordan couldn't help himself. He broke away from Oz and hurried to meet his father. That was what Oz loved most about the kid. He truly loved the man who was not his biological father. He loved him as if he was.

"Hey Dad," Jordan said as he approached Alex.

"Hey, Champ," Alex said as he placed his arm around Jordan and hurried with him toward the car. "Mom's okay?"

"Yes, sir."

"You saw her with your own two eyes?"

"Yes, sir. Oz had my security detail take me to her when we heard about that shooting. She wanted to see me and I wanted to see her.

She's okay."

Alex exhaled. "Good. And Angie?"

"She's with Auntie Faye. She took her to one of their friends' children's parties and kept her after they heard about the shooting."

"And Jovani?"

"She's with her mother," said Jordan, "all I know."

Alex nodded. Jovani was his daughter Cate's child. His one and only grandchild. They all were on his mind. But Kari most of all. He and Jordan hurried to the Bentley.

"Hello Alexio," said Oz in his best Greek accent. He always laid it on thick when he saw his brother.

But Alex had one thing on his mind. He started looking into the Bentley. Then he frowned and looked at Oz. "She's okay, then where is she?"

"The doctor is checking her out," said Oz.

"*The doctor*? I thought you told me--"

"She is fine. I told you right. It's just that Diallo wanted her checked out," he added hesitantly. "She wanted to come, but Diallo insisted she stay."

Alex frowned. That wasn't their family physician's name. "Who's Diallo?"

"He's Kari's business partner, or potential partner. They were having a meeting at the mall when it happened. I overheard him mention that he and Kari might purchase that mall."

Alex looked at Oz as if he was talking gibberish. What business partner? What meeting? What *mall*? "Where is she?"

"She's at his chateau."

Alex frowned. "*What*?"

"He has a world-renowned medical team that travels with him. He wanted them to check her out."

"And you left my wife at some man's chateau, and with a man I've never met face to face in my life?"

"It's not like that, brother. He's . . ."

"He's what?"

"He's a very successful businessman. As rich as you are. Or nearly."

"And that's supposed to make me feel better?"

"No, but . . ."

"But what?"

"But he saved her life, Alexio. She was standing right beside Rho Scotts. He got hit. She didn't. He saved her life."

That definitely cooled Alex's perspective about the man. But still!

"And besides," Oz added again, "she's not alone by any means. I left one of our security details there with her. I've been getting constant updates. She's fine, Alexio. She's fine."

Alex didn't know what to make of any of it. But he knew he had some tough questions for Oz.

He looked at Jordan. "I want you to go home," he said. Then before Jordan could object, he looked at his security detail chief. "Rick!"

Rick hurried over. "Sir?"

"Take my son home."

"Yes, sir."

"But I want to go back to Mom," Jordan complained.

But Alex had already gotten into the Bentley, Oz had already gotten in on the driver side behind the wheel, and they were driving away.

"Come on, Jordan," said Rick, who could feel the kid's pain, as he and Jordan headed to the detail car.

And once again, Jordan felt like he used to feel when Money, the man he and his mother used to live with, would harass him nonstop. He felt as if he wasn't a part of the family at all, but an interloper on the outside trying to get in. Like he was a nonfactor. Always excluded from the important family matters. Like he was the one that didn't matter.

He got in the backseat of the car, and turtled.

CHAPTER SIXTEEN

As Oz drove Alex to go see his wife, Alex hesitated before asking the question he dreaded asking. But knew he had to. "Is this Diallo person a tall black guy? Good looking?"

"Tall black guy and *great* looking, yes," said Oz. Then he glanced over at his brother. "What? You think you know him?"

Alex didn't respond to that. He was still fuming that Oz nor Kari had bothered to mention this man to him before now. "Have you met him before today?"

"Never," said Oz as he drove. Then he glanced at his brother again. "Why are you worrying so much? She's not alone with the guy, if that's what's bothering you. I ordered Doc to get over to the chateau too. He's with Kari as well. Not even Dee's medical team can run a single test without Doc's approval." He looked over at Alex again. "I'm not going to leave your wife vulnerable ever. You know me. And like I said, the guy saved her life."

"If he didn't set that whole thing up himself," Alex murmured.

But Oz heard him. And was astounded by what he heard. "He set up a mass shooting?

Come on, brother! Why on earth would you even think that?"

"You said yourself he was looking to purchase that mall. What better leverage for purchase than damaged goods? What better leverage for purchase than a place where a mass shooting had just taken place?"

"People died, Alex," Oz said angrily. "Including a girl I knew. That shit wasn't staged!"

"Maybe it got out of hand. You don't know that."

"You don't either!"

Alex exhaled. Then he looked over at Oz. "Who was she?"

Oz looked out of the driver side window. It still hurt. "Girl named Jill. We used to be tight before I hooked up with Glo."

"One of your fuck partners?"

"Don't demean her like that!"

Alex exhaled. "You're right. I apologize." Then he leaned his head back.

Oz looked at Alex. "You didn't get the deal signed, did you?"

Alex hesitated. "No. I heard Kari was involved in a mass shooting and no way was I hanging around to sign papers." Especially with the nonstarter of a deal Bev had on the table.

"No deal. Great. Wait until the Street hears about this. I told Zeke to tell you she was alright. I started not to even call you, but I knew you'd kick my ass if you found out from any other source."

"And you would have been correct," said Alex. "You think I'm going to hear my wife was involved in a mass shooting and I decide to hang around for a meeting?"

"A meeting that can save your conglomerate, yes."

"Then you don't know me at all."

"I don't know if any of us do anymore."

Alex looked at his brother. "What's that supposed to mean?"

"This has been a crazy-ass year, Alexio. You're hardly ever home. Kari feels neglected. Jordan feels alienated. Angela barely knows your ass. This year you've been more absent than I have! And I understand the reason, I truly do. I know your empire has had another rough year, and I know even that's an understatement. But I can count on my two hands how many weeks you've been home without having to leave town to deal with some new crisis."

"You think I was leaving on purpose?"

"I think you could have let some of your senior people do more."

"And they would have handled more if every one of those crises weren't on my level. But they were on my level. And there was no farming that shit out. I had to handle it myself."

But Alex was thinking about Kari and this new "partner" of hers. "Why would he need to travel with a medical team?" he asked.

"According to him, he doesn't like hospitals either. If he gets ill, he doesn't want anybody touching him except his own personal physicians. He's a billionaire. Almost as big as Dangote in Nigeria. Which means he's eccentric. You guys always have some crazy quirks anyway. A traveling medical team is apparently his."

"I don't have any crazy quirks," said Alex.

Oz looked at him. "That's what you think."

But Alex had Kari on his mind. He exhaled and ran his hand across his face. "Just get me to my wife," he said.

But it was the way he said it, as if Oz was responsible for what happened, that angered Oz. "Why are you jumping all over my case? I didn't do this to her. I was there. I wasn't the one in New York. I was right there with her. You're the one who hasn't been paying attention. Not me!"

Alex looked at Oz.

"Know how many times she's met with Diallo? At least ten times. Maybe even a dozen times. And over several months they've been meeting."

Alex knew they had been having dinner dates. His security guy acknowledged that. But to hear Oz say it made it sound even worse than he had originally thought.

"Did you hear me, Alexio? They've been like bosom buddies for months now. And you knew nothing about it."

Alex frowned. "Why would I need to know about it? She's handling a business transaction. I don't follow her ass toe to toe."

"You'd better start if you want to keep her."

Alex didn't expect to hear that. He looked at his brother. "What's with you and all of these innuendos, Odysseus?"

"All I'm saying is stop acting as if these men out here don't want your wife. Because newsflash: they do. Plenty of them do. And if your busy ass isn't careful," Oz added, but didn't say anymore.

He didn't have to. Alex got the point. And it was a worry on top of an already mountain of worries he had to deal with. But all he wanted right now was to eyeball Kari. He had to see her for himself. Then he'd know the deal. "Can't you drive this thing any faster?" he asked his already speeding brother.

"You're the one that bought it for her.

Bentleys are cute. They never said they were fast."

"Just go," said Alex.

And Oz, as he usually did, obliged the boss.

CHAPTER SEVENTEEN

They arrived at the Pensacola mansion, hopped out of the Bentley, and with Alex leading the charge, they hurried inside.

Alex saw his security detail guys there, and the family physician once he walked inside, but it was Kari he had to eyeball. And when he saw her, sitting as if she was the woman of the house with her back against the armrest and her feet propped up, a glass of wine in her hand, it gave him some pause. But only for half a second. He hurried on over to her and sat on the edge of the sofa beside her. "Hey," he said.

She smiled, but it seemed strained to him. "Hey Alex. You didn't have to come back."

"You're okay then?"

"Oh yes, I'm good. They gave me a thorough workover. I just got a little bruise right here," she showed him the backside of her arm. "But other than that, I'm okay."

But Alex could see the strain in her large eyes. He pulled her into his arms.

Oz stood there staring at Kari as her husband held her. Her eyes were squeezed shut, but he couldn't tell if it was because she loved Alex's embrace, or was regretful and would prefer it had been Diallo's arms around her. It wasn't until they stopped embracing and she opened her eyes did Oz get a good read on Kari's feelings. And when he saw Kari give Alex that look of love she gave to no one else, Oz actually exhaled. He felt much better! Alex was still her knight.

But that didn't mean Diallo wasn't.

Two things could be true at the same time, Oz knew.

"I'm okay, Alex, honest I am," said Kari when Alex continued to look her over.

"Why didn't you go to a hospital?"

"You know why. I hate those places. And I told everybody I was fine. And all those tests they ran bore me out."

"Thank God," a deep, African-accented voice said and everybody looked in the direction of the sound.

It was Diallo. He had just come into the living room. And as soon as Alex saw him, he saw that his beauty, and sexuality on top of it, was obvious. The fact that he could easily be Kari's type was obvious too. And he had such a devastatingly charming smile, even from across the room. He was extending his hand as he approached. "Mr. Drakos, I presume," Diallo said as Alex stood up and they shook hands.

"Mister?" Alex asked.

117

"Koffi. Diallo Koffi. But please call me Dee."

"I understand you assisted my wife."

"He did more than assist me, Alex," said Kari. "He saved my life."

"Thank you," Alex said, heartfelt.

"You are welcome. It was my pleasure," he said and smiled at Kari.

"We're going into business together," Kari said.

Alex looked at her. "Oh yeah?"

"That's why we were at the mall."

Diallo looked at her. "So you see it as a definite possibility?" he asked her.

"Most definitely," said Kari. "Especially with the number of black businesses we can help."

Diallo smiled that alluring smile again. "I knew you would see the beauty in it," he said as if he was seeing the beauty in her too.

Alex saw it too. In the way Diallo was looking at his wife. And he'd had enough. He looked at their family physician, who was also in the room. "She's good?"

"Yes, sir. There are no issues whatsoever beyond that small bruise she pointed out to you."

Then Alex looked at his wife. "Ready?"

Kari didn't expect to be so abruptly carted

off, but she knew Alex. Time was always money with him. "Yes, I'm ready," she said, getting up. Alex helped her to her feet.

She handed the glass of wine to Diallo. "Thank you so much for hosting me until my husband got back in town."

"Any time" he said. "But certainly not under these circumstances," he added, and Kari nodded her definite agreement.

"Goodbye," said Kari.

"Let me know once you're ready to resume our talks."

"When will you need to know my decision?"

"Yesterday," said Diallo. "But tomorrow will have to do. Which, under the circumstances, sounds crass I know. But life goes on, you see."

Kari knew. "Right," she said.

"We can perhaps meet up at that diner, at Gloria's Place, in the morning? Around ten?"

"That can work," said Kari, they said their goodbyes, and they all walked outside.

The security chief on site got behind the wheel of Kari's Bentley. Kari got on the backseat. But before Oz could get in, Alex pulled him aside.

"I want the deepest background on this guy, you hear me? I'm talking from his babyhood up."

"I've already ordered it," said Oz. "On the surface everything checks out, but you never know until you go into the deep blue sea of his life. That's where shit happens."

"Right."

Oz could tell his brother was worried. Or was he scared? "What are your impressions?"

"Slick. Smart. A nice guy."

"On the surface."

"Right."

"What are your impressions of Kari's impression of him?" Oz asked.

Alex was offended by the question. He never discussed the intricacies of his marriage with anybody. "Make sure they go deep," was all he'd say as he turned to get to the Bentley.

"And Alexio?"

"Yeah?" Alex said without turning around.

"This chateau? She's been here before."

When Alex heard those words, he turned around. "Who's been here before?"

"Your wife."

To say Alex was shocked was an understatement. Business meetings were one thing. But why in hell did she need to go to his house? He looked away from Oz for a second, then nodded his understanding. And then he got in the back passenger seat beside Kari, while Oz got in up front with the driver. Kari leaned her small body against Alex's large one when he got in, and he placed his arm around her. And they rode home in peace.

But there was nothing, for either of them, peaceful about it.

CHAPTER EIGHTEEN

They sat in the tub for nearly an hour. Kari sat between Alex's legs, with her back against his back, while Alex had his back against the tub. And they sipped champagne and tried to relax. Alex was fondling Kari between her legs, to soothe her, and Kari was leaned back, her eyes closed, enjoying the massage. It had been a harrowing day for both of them. But especially for Kari. She could still hear those gunshots ringing in her ear, and the sounds of screams that echoed throughout that massive mall when people realized it wasn't fireworks or some other simple explanation. They ran for their lives.

Kari also knew she could have lost hers had it not been for Dee.

Alex knew it too. It was sticking to him like indigestion. But his gratitude kept him from being jealous. The man saved Kari's life. He would forever owe him one.

But he couldn't deal with that right now. Even though Kari wasn't physically harmed, every now and then he could see creases of worry appear on her forehead, as if she was re-living it all over again. As if emotionally she didn't get out unscathed.

He stopped fondling her and lifted her naked body up onto the center of his lap. And right away, Kari could feel why he lifted her there. He already had a rock-hard erection. And when he eased it inside of her, and that feeling just his touch gave to her returned, she groaned in satisfaction.

Alex went easy on her. For nearly half an hour he did her slow and easy. He was doing her so gently that she wanted to melt into him it felt so good. He kept both of them on the verge of cumming for nearly the entire time he was inside of her. It took skill and mastery to pull that off, and Alex, Kari knew, had tons of both. Nobody could do her better.

But for a brief moment, she found herself wondering if Diallo could.

Her eyes flew open when she realized what she was thinking. How could she have thought such a thing!

Alex was no stranger to sensual thoughts. To seeing a gorgeous woman and wondering what she'd be like beneath him. When Kari's eyes flew open, and her body reacted too, he knew exactly what had gone down. And he'd be lying if he said it didn't scare him. Because it did.

Not since Kari's infatuation with Jordan's

123

biological father did he ever feel that scared. He could lose Kari? It wasn't possible. But if it wasn't, why was his ass trembling?

And it angered him. After all he did for her she'd have some wet dream about some other guy? And just like that, his slow and easy lovemaking became another branding session. He began to pound her. He stared at her gorgeous face as he put that good hurting on her he knew she loved. He had to remind her who he was. And whose she was. He had to remind himself that no way would she ever give up what he put on her. Not ever.

Kari had been with Alex long enough to know the difference between him making love to her versus branding her again. But she loved it. She loved that branding as much as he loved putting it on her. And she began to cry out in joy when her orgasm began. Because she knew it was going to be electrifying.

And it was. His branding caused her to cum far harder than his easy lovemaking would have. And her cumming caused him to cum. And it was a hard, wonderful, achingly beautiful cum for him too.

That was why, in the mist of his orgasm, he leaned Kari's head back and began kissing her, just as hard as they were cumming, on her lips. Now she was groaning in his mouth.

Later, when it was all over, they stayed where they were for several minutes. Kari was waiting for Alex to talk about it. But like most things lately, he didn't say a word. Which disappointed her. She was tired of being the one to have to bring up their problems as if he had no clue they had any. So she got out of the tub, dried off, and took herself to bed.

And that elephant in the room, along with all those other elephants in all those other rooms, remained right where it shouldn't have been.

Later that same day, Walter Vokos, the Chief Financial Officer for Alex's European southeastern sector, walked to the car inside his home's garage, pressed the Start button, and then heard the sizzle. Before he realized what that sizzle was, his car exploded into a fireball of wreckage that took out the powerful CFO, and his garage and house, right along with him.

CHAPTER NINETEEN

The next morning, Kari was seated at the kitchen table eating breakfast with Jordan and Angela. Although Angela was playing a game on her little cell phone more than she was eating, Kari was more concerned about Jordan. He'd seemed as out of sorts as she seemed lately.

"How are your classes going?" she asked him.

Jordan was eating his bacon, but wasn't tasting a thing. "Okay."

"Your debate team ready for the semis?"

"We're getting there. You coming?"

"Absolutely."

Jordan looked at his mother. "Dad coming?"

Kari looked her son in the eye. It used to just be the two of them. And one thing she never did was lie to him. "Did you ask him?"

"Yes."

"What did he tell you?"

"He got a phone call and told me he'd talk to me later. And later never comes."

Kari exhaled. She knew what he meant. "It's been a tough year," Kari started saying.

126

But Jordan was already shaking his head. "Don't even, Ma."

Kari frowned. "Don't even what?"

"Don't make excuses for him!" Even little Angela looked up when her big brother raised his voice.

But Jordan continued. "We used to be a family. All of us. We used to do things together. But now it's just me, you, and Angie doing things together. And then there's Dad. It's like we don't matter to him anymore. It's like *I* don't matter. I wanted to come back to that house where you were after Oz and I picked Dad up from the airport, but Dad wouldn't let me. He made his security people take me home. Do you know how that made me feel? I had just as much right to be there with you as he did. But he treats me like a child. Like I'm not . . ."

"Like you're not what?" Kari asked him.

But Jordan wouldn't say. Because he knew, like Kari knew, it spoke for itself. And Kari wasn't going to place her hand on his hand and comfort him. She wasn't going to placate him. He was too smart for that. "He can do better, yes, he can."

"Then why don't you make him?"

Kari frowned. "Make him? Jordan, how am I going to make a grown-ass man do anything he doesn't want to do? I'm tired of this shit too. You think I'm not tired of it?"

"But what are you doing about it?" Jordan asked her bluntly.

"What do you suggest I do about it, Jordan?"

"Leave!" Jordan said forcefully. "Before it gets bad like Money."

Kari's heart dropped. Was that what he was thinking? "*Oh, Jordan,*" she said with an ache in her voice as she removed her napkin from her lap and sat it on the table. Then she got up and went over to her son, giving him a hug where he sat. "It'll never be like that again, baby. Daddy's nothing like that."

"But Money wasn't like that, either, until he was like that. And I don't want you going through that again. It's not fair to you. It's not fair to Angie. And it's not fair to me."

Kari rubbed her son's soft hair and closed her eyes. She knew Alex's neglect was affecting her. And intellectually she knew it was affecting their children. But to hear it from her child did something to her. She knelt down to where she was face to face with her still-seated son. "You listen to me, Jordan Drakos. No matter what Daddy and I are going through, he loves you. He's nothing like Money. He just works too hard. That's his sin."

"But you don't know that. You don't know

what he's doing in all those different cities and countries he's always going to. Guys at school be talking about they heard he was with this woman and that woman."

"They been saying that for years," said Kari. "You know that's a bunch of bull."

"I don't know anything anymore. He's not like he used to be. I don't recognize him anymore. And when guys get like that it usually means a girl is involved."

Kari wasn't trying to hear that. Not even from Jordan. "Just finish your breakfast," she said, and went back to her seat.

She and Jordan exchanged a glance, as if he knew it crossed her mind too, but Kari wasn't trying to entertain that. She and Alex had enough real problems with just being present in each other's lives. She wasn't going to invent problems too.

"Daddy! Daddy!" Angela jumped up from the table as Kari and Jordan looked where she was running.

Alex, fully dressed in suit and tie, had come downstairs and was heading into the kitchen. He grabbed Angela at a full run and hoisted her into the air. "There's my Speedy Gonzales!"

"I won, Daddy. I won the game."

"Again?"

"It's my fourth time."

"Good on you! Maybe I'll give it a try one of these days."

Angela said nothing to that. He'd made that promise too many times. He carried her over to the table.

"Good morning," he said and as soon as she said it, Jordan jumped up and grabbed his bookbag.

"Bye Ma," he said, kissing Kari on the cheeks.

"Drive carefully, Jordan."

"Yes, ma'am. Come on, Ang," he said as he took her out of his father's arms. He was driving her to her country day school before he drove himself to Dreston.

"Good morning," Alex said to Jordan. But Jordan didn't respond. He took his baby sister and headed for the exit.

Alex watched them leave, and then walked over to the table. "What's his problem?"

"You," Kari said.

Alex looked at her. "Me?"

Kari got up from her seat. "I'll fix you a plate," she said as Alex sat down.

When she returned with his breakfast and sat it in front of him, then sat back down at her own plate, they ate in silence for several minutes.

Until Alex finally looked over at Kari. "You were at his house before?" he asked her.

Kari's first instinct was to ask whose house, but she knew exactly who Alex was talking about. And if he was asking the question, it was because he knew the answer. "Yes."

"Why?"

He asked it matter-of-factly, but his eyes showed emotion. He didn't like it one bit, and Kari knew he didn't. "He invited me over."

"Why?"

"I told you we were having meetings to determine if we were a good fit to become business partners."

"I've been in my line of work for decades. You know how many potential business partners I've invited to my house?"

"He's not you."

"I know that," said Alex. "But does he?"

That insult hit Kari to her core. "How dare you make a comment like that! Of course he knows he's not my husband, which was what you were implying!"

"What does he want from you?"

"He's putting together a group of African-American investors to help black-owned small businesses. That mall was going to be the first investment with a proviso that half of the businesses be black-owned. And I want in on that."

"You are in business," said Alex. "You're in through me."

"I want to do my own thing, Alex. I need to do my own thing."

"And why's that?"

"Because I'm not happy anymore!" Kari said it out loud for the first time.

It stunned Alex. He could only stare at her.

"I'm not fulfilled anymore," Kari continued. "I don't feel valued. I don't feel useful. I go to work, I get my work done, but it's like I'm phoning it in. And I'll relationship is in bits and pieces. I see you for a minute, we make love, and then you're gone again. What kind of relationship is that? And it's affecting Jordan too."

"Jordan?"

"Yes! He's as invested in you as I am. And he's not getting any return on his investment either."

Kari could tell Alex was taking what she'd just said hard. But his expression didn't let her know if he agreed with what she had said, or disagreed vehemently. With Alex, it was never easy to tell.

"You are unhappy?" he asked her as if

that was really the only thing he truly heard.

Kari hated admitting it herself. "Yes," she said. "And maybe it's just that I'm burned out or getting older or just plain tired, but I'm not happy with how things are going with us."

"You know I've got business issues to resolve---"

"It's not just right now, Alex, and you know that. Every single year we go through this shit. You do good, then you do bad. It's a cycle with you. And every year it's gotten progressively worse. Every single year. Now even Jordan's seeing it. And I can't have that."

Alex knew it too. He ran his hand across his face. "What do you propose we do about it?" he asked her. "Therapy?"

"I'm done talking," said Kari bluntly. "We've been talking about this year after year after year after year and nothing changes."

"It does change."

"And then it goes right back how it was again, which means that change ain't shit! I can't keep putting myself through this. And now our children too?" She shook her head. "I can't do it anymore. I'm not doing it anymore."

Before Alex could even think of a way to respond to such a statement, the intercom buzzed. He angrily pressed the button. "What?"

"Sorry to disturb you, sir, but Mr. Coles is

here to see you."

Griffin Coles, called Griff, was the chief of security for all of the Drakos Corporation's assets. As powerful as the CFO, he was a very busy man. Which meant it was bad news for him to be paying Alex a visit that early in the day. But Alex just sat there. Griff represented exactly what Kari was talking about: a faucet that never turned off. And Alex knew it.

But Kari also knew Alex was chomping at the bit to find out why Griff would be there. She pressed the intercom button herself. "Send him up," she said, and released the button.

Kari began standing up with her half-eaten plate of food in her hand. "I've got a meeting to get to," she said as she headed for the kitchen sink. By the time she scraped her own plate and placed it in the dishwasher, and then went and retrieved and then scraped her children's plates, Griffin Coles, a stocky built black man, was ringing the bell.

Kari answered the front door, gave Griff a hug, told him where Alex was, and then left. Griff made his way into the kitchen.

"Hope I didn't interrupt anything," Griff said as he stood at the table.

"Your timing is lousy, Griff. What is it?"

"You haven't touched your food."

Alex looked at Griff as if he knew he'd

better get on with it. And Griff did. "Walter Vokos was found dead this morning."

Alex looked at Griff. "Dead as in natural causes?"

"Dead as in murdered. A car bomb in his garage."

"I'll be damn. His family harmed?"

Griff nodded. "They were inside the house. Nothing survived that explosion."

Alex leaned his head back.

"That's what his ass get for stealing your money and trying to blame it on Galani."

"What did his family do? They didn't have shit to do with his crimes." Then Alex exhaled. "Any new news on Galani?"

Griff shook his head. "Nothing. We still got nothing. Those assholes either buried her already, or they're hiding her in plain sight. One of the two."

"Find out who's behind Walt's murder. Although I'm reasonably certain it was those same vultures that stole my money."

"Dave Pantanzis?"

"And his crew at Southeast, yes."

"Refresh my memory. Why haven't we fired all of those bastards yet?"

"Because I want my company restored first. They've already taken all there is to take, save a measly seventeen percent. I need them close to see what their next moves will be."

Then he looked at Griff. "I ordered security teams to watch all of them."

"Right," said Griff. "And they are watching all of them."

"But nobody saw that car bomb getting planted in the man's garage?"

"The team we had watching Walt was murdered too. They took them out before they planted the bomb."

This surprised Alex.

Griff noticed his surprise. "What is it?"

"I want our people to look beyond Dave Pantanzis. There's no way he would have that kind of reach to outflank our own guys."

"What are you thinking? He's answering to somebody else?"

Alex nodded. "That's exactly what I'm thinking."

"You think Walt found out about it?"

"I don't know. But we need to find out. This might go well beyond that group at Southeast."

"Don't tell me that!"

"Look into it."

"I'll have our people on it immediately. But . . ."

"But what?"

"I know this is a sticky subject for you,

Alex. But don't you think it's time we call in Oz on this?"

"I do not want Odysseus involved at all. He's trying to leave his past behind, and I want to keep it that way."

Griff stared at Alex. Surely he knew Oz wasn't just in the mob, but was one of the most powerful mob bosses in the south. But yet he refused to see it. Nobody was able to compartmentalize better than Alex. "Believe it or not," he said, "Walter Vokos isn't the main reason I'm here."

Alex looked at him. Was he kidding? "What's the main reason?"

"Bev is back in Budapest."

"Ah shit!" Alex said loudly and slammed his hand on the table. "I thought she was still in New York."

"She was. Until she wasn't. But the good news is she's still willing to deal. She wouldn't tell me the terms, but she said you know the terms."

Alex didn't respond to that. Beverly Norgate's terms were never something anybody would mention. "And the bad news?"

"That window is closing fast. Paige met with me this morning. She said if we're going to make a move, we've got to make that move now. And you've got to get her to yes. Not maybe. Not halfway. All the way yes. Or we're through. Our stock is tanking again this morning and the longer this drags out the more we'll lose. We're at the end of the road. No last-minute reprieves this time. Bev is all we have."

Alex was so angry he grabbed that plate of food in front of him and threw it against the wall, shattering the plate and scattering the food.

Griff was aghast, but he was not surprised. Nobody wanted the future of their entire empire to come down to Bev Norgate.

Nobody.

CHAPTER TWENTY

Kari was in her office at The Drakos hotel downstairs, seated behind her desk, when Alex walked in. It didn't take a rocket scientist to know what he wanted. "Where this time?" she asked him.

He placed his hands in his pockets. "Budapest. Hungary."

Kari shook her head. *That far*, she wanted to complain. But she held her peace.

Alex saw the disappointment on her pretty face. "It can't be helped," he said.

"It never can," she said.

And it caused Alex to sigh out loud. Because she was right. It was the family or his empire. He no longer seemed capable of having both. But he couldn't deal with that right now.

He leaned down and kissed Kari on the lips. Kari closed her eyes. She still loved that man with a love that she knew was killing her.

Because she was the only one making all the sacrifices. Because she was the only one who seemed to realize just how threadbare their marriage truly was.

When he stopped kissing her and she opened her eyes, he was staring into them. And his heart was heavy. He loved her so much! But he knew a part of him took her for granted because she loved him too. And he knew it. "Maybe when I get back in town we can---"

But Kari cut him off. "Tell me no lies," she said to him in a harsh tone and stared him in the face.

That look cut Alex short. He'd never seen a more determined look on Kari's face in all the time he'd known her. And it spooked him.

"You don't want to be late," she said as she continued to give him that hard, cold stare. "That ain't your thing."

Alex felt like it was winter in September. He hated that he had to leave. They had shit to work through and he knew it! But he also knew, if he was going to keep his companies cobbled together, he had to go. There was no longer any choice in the matter. He had to leave.

He'd just have to work it out when he got back.

He gave Kari another kiss, although she turned her mouth away, leaving him only with her silk-smooth cheek. But he took that and kissed her there. Then he walked right out of that door.

As soon as he did, Kari covered her mouth with her hand, as her lip began to tremble. And then, as if the buildup had been building up for years, tears began to slowly, but assuredly, slide down her face.

He left anyway.

He left anyway.

He left her.

Anyway.

CHAPTER TWENTY-ONE

"Good morning," she said as she and Diallo hugged. "I know I'm late."

"I factor it in now."

Kari looked at Diallo strangely as she sat across from him in his booth. They were at Glo's Place and the breakfast crowd had already thinned out. Which, they both knew, was a good time to meet. But what had he factored in? "Excuse me?"

"When I am meeting you anywhere, I factor in the fact that you will be at least fifteen minutes late. Therefore, I arrive ten minutes late. I only have to wait on you, on average, five minutes. I factor your lateness in now."

Kari shook her head. It didn't use to be this way. Seemed as if she wasn't herself in any area of her life lately. It had to change!

"I also took the liberty of ordering you a cup of coffee. Cream with sugar. Two lumps or clumps or however you phrase it."

Kari smiled a weak smile. "Thanks."

But Diallo could see she wasn't in the best of moods. "Where is Odysseus? I thought your husband would not allow you to go anywhere without him."

"Oz is in Philly visiting his wife and daughter."

"In Philadelphia? Why are they in Philadelphia?"

"That's where Gloria's from. Whenever they have issues, she goes home to daddy. It's so common that it's considered a part of their routine."

"It would not be a part of my routine. Unless, of course, I loved the woman." He smiled. "Then all bets were off."

Kari tried to smile too. But it was an even weaker attempt.

Diallo noticed it again. "You are usually happier when we meet. What is wrong, Karena?"

She sighed. "Just still getting over yesterday I guess."

"Ah. Yesterday. It was my first experience with the American mass shootings."

Kari wished it was her first.

"How is your friend, Mr. Scotts?"

"Rho's doing well," Kari said, nodding. "He's coming along better than expected, thank God."

"Good to hear," Diallo said. And then he found himself staring at Kari as she began speaking glowingly of her accountant's recovery. What he'd give to have her speaking

143

glowingly of him. "And you, my dear? How are you?"

Kari smiled. "I'm okay."

"Not very good, Karena, at putting on."

Kari looked at him. He saw her. He listened to her. He paid attention to her. But so did Alex in the beginning. But it still felt good to have somebody's attention. No, she thought to herself. Not somebody. Diallo. It felt good to have Diallo's attention. He seemed like such a nice guy.

"I shall ask again," he said, and this time he reached over and placed both of Kari's small dark hands into his large dark hands. "How. Are. You, Karena?"

This time Kari smiled, but it was a genuine smile. "I'm better now that I'm around your happy face. And my answer is yes. I will join your investment group. I am onboard."

Diallo made a point to smile that piercingly mesmerizing smile. "We will be grand partners together, Karena. I promise you that."

He squeezed Kari's hands affectionately, and Kari was surprised that she didn't mind. He would put her on a pedestal, she was certain of it. But would he put her there and leave her there, unattended and growing old alone, like Alex was in danger of doing? Or was he truly different?

"Kari."

She removed her hand from Diallo's hand as soon as she heard that voice. They had done nothing wrong. But hearing that soft, sweet voice of Alex's reminded her that thoughts did count for something too. What was she thinking?

She and Diallo both looked up and saw that Alex was standing at their booth. And all she could see in his eyes were a combination of shock and disappointment. And sadness.

Kari felt a little disappointed in herself. Because she was beginning to enjoy Diallo's touch, and she knew it. "What are you doing here?" she asked her husband.

"To get you. You're coming with me."

"Whoa," said Diallo, as if he had some standing in the matter. "You are sounding as if you are ordering her about. You cannot do that. That is not cool, my friend."

"First of all I'm not your friend," Alex said.

"He didn't mean," Kari started to say because she knew when Alex was getting heated.

But Alex wasn't getting heated. He was already there. "And second of all," he said, ignoring Kari, "who the fuck are you to tell me what I can or cannot do with my own wife?"

"All I was saying, and saying with

respect," said Diallo, "is that your command sounded, not like a suggestion, but like an order."

"It is an order."

"But that is not right. I know you are far older than she is."

"Dee don't go there," said Kari.

"But she is not a child. She is a woman."

"Yes, she is. My woman." Alex looked Diallo head on. "And you'd be wise not to forget that."

Diallo stood on his feet. Alex and Kari's bodyguards, who were nearby in the diner, stood up too. Diallo's bodyguard, who was likewise in the diner, stood up as well.

But Kari would have none of it. "Dee, sit down. What are you doing?"

"You do not deserve to call her your woman," Diallo said to Alex. "You are not worthy to call her your woman."

Alex frowned. "You better get out of my face, motherfucker."

Diallo frowned. "Who are you calling a motherfucker?"

"You motherfucker!"

Diallo, now so angry and loaded with testosterone-fueled embarrassment, leaned back and attempted to punch Alex with the hardest punch in his arsenal. But Alex saw it coming a mile away and easily ducked. But the idea that he would have even attempted it, caused Alex's anger to unleash and he unloaded on Diallo. And there was no ducking Alex's punch as he punched Diallo so hard that Diallo was knocked back onto the table of the booth behind them. The customers nearby hurriedly moved out of the way.

Diallo's bodyguard hurried to assist him. Alex and Kari's bodyguards were grinning, and knew to stay put.

Kari got up angry at both men. But especially, and to Diallo's surprise, she was more angry at him! "What's wrong with you?" she asked him. "I told you to sit down. I told you to leave it alone."

"And that gives him a license to plummet someone?" Diallo's bodyguard helped him back on his feet.

But Kari wasn't buying it. "You started this shit, Dee. You threw a punch at him. Because yours didn't land, is that his fault too?"

"Okay. On that you are correct. I apologize."

"Keep it!" Alex said angrily. "Let's go, Karena."

"You do not have to obey him."

"Stop that, Dee, now I mean it! This has nothing to do with you."

"He is a selfish, domineering man who does not care a twit about you!"

"Didn't I tell you to stay out of this?" Kari had had it now. "You're taking this shit too far."

"But he does not own you."

Kari frowned. "This is my husband, what are you talking about? It has nothing to do with ownership. Nothing!" Then she pointed at Diallo because she saw in that moment that he was just another man trying to possess her too. "Mind your own damn business," she said to him and then grabbed her purse and headed for the exit.

Alex looked at Diallo too. "Stay away from my wife."

"Your wife doesn't appear to want to stay away from me," Diallo responded.

Alex knew it wasn't a lie, so he didn't take it any further. He just left.

"You okay, sir?" asked Diallo's bodyguard.

"I am fine," Diallo said as he watched Kari and Alex, along with their bodyguards, leave the diner. When he saw Alex and Kari get into Alex's limousine, he grabbed his phone, sat back down, and then pressed a familiar number.

"It's now or never," he said without waiting for any response. And ended the call.

CHAPTER TWENTY-TWO

The ride to the airfield was a quiet ride. Alex took hold of Kari's hand and kept it as they rode, and he could feel the tension ease up. But it was still there. And to make matters worse the very song Kari used to always hum when they first met, Tracy Chapman's *Fast Car*, was playing on the stereo inside the limousine. And it made it all just feel so sad.

"You got a fast car.
I want a ticket to anywhere.
Maybe we make a deal.
Maybe together we can get somewhere.
Anyplace is better.
Starting from zero, got nothing to lose.
Maybe we'll make something.
Me myself, I got nothing to prove."

Alex gripped Kari's hand tighter as the somberness of the song took them back to that time when Alex invited Kari to go on a dinner date with him all the way to New York City, and she was afraid to go. It was so out of her comfort zone that she almost said no way. But she got on his private plane with him anyway. The best decision she ever made. And it all had come to this?

"You got a fast car.
Is it fast enough so we can fly away?
We gotta make a decision.
Leave tonight or live and die this way."

Kari made that decision and went with Alex. Now she had a different decision to make, and so did he. And it was tearing them both apart.

After the song ended, and several miles later, Kari spoke. "How long will you be gone this time?"

Alex wished he could be more certain. But he wasn't going to tell her any lies. "I don't know. I have to get this merger done or I'm in trouble."

"You'll find a way. You always do."

Alex looked at Kari. Her response triggered him. Maybe it was her answer. Maybe it was the fact that she was sitting at that table holding that bastard's hand. Maybe it was the fact that while he was making love to her, she thought about that same guy. He didn't know. But it pissed him off. "What kind of answer is that? I tell you I'm in trouble and you dismiss it like it's nothing?"

"That's not what I did."

"I know I haven't been here for you lately. I understand that. But you haven't exactly been bouncing off the walls for me either. Emotionally, I might have checked out, but you've checked out too. This shit cuts both ways, Karena. I hope you realize that."

Kari was staring at Alex. She hadn't realized it at all. But she refused to let him lay his shit at her feet. "If I did check out," she said, "it would have been for a reason. Because I counted it up."

Alex frowned. "Counted what up?"

"In the last twelve months you've been at home a total of two-and-a-half months. That's all. In an entire year, Alex. Two-and-a-half months total. And you don't expect that to do our marriage any harm? Let my ass pull that shit."

Alex was stunned to hear that number, but he knew they still could work it out. But they would have to keep all third parties out of the picture. "I don't want you to have anything more to do with Diallo Koffi," he said.

Another deflection. "What does he have to do with this?"

"You heard me."

"No you aren't trying to make this all about him."

"Did you hear me? I don't want you to have anything more to do with him. Understand?"

Kari just shook her head in disgust.

"Do you hear me, Karena?"

"Yes! I hear you." Then she looked angrily at him. "Now you hear me." Tears began to well up in her big, bright eyes, which was another shocker for Alex. Kari was not a crier.

But Kari was serious. He saw that too. "I will not continue to live like this, Alex. There is no way in hell I'm going to keep living like this. You have got to make a choice. I'm sorry, but you do. Either you run your empire and all of the ups and downs and loses and gains and you're going to lose the conglomerate if you don't get this deal or that deal or that other deal done. You can have all that. But if these past years have taught us anything, it has taught us that you can't have both. You can't have your empire and me too. It's not working and we can't make it work. Bottom line."

Alex's longtime driver glanced through the rearview mirror. Even he could feel the gravity of what Kari was saying.

But Kari kept going. "You've tried to juggle both of us. You've tried to invest more time with the family. And it worked for a minute.

But that was the exception, not the rule. That shit was temporary. But I'm not doing it. I'm not going to be your side piece that you give scant attention to when it suits your ass. Ain't happening. That shit's done. I'll be by myself before I live like this another day!"

Alex just sat there. His heart was hammering. "What are you saying, Karena?" he asked, and then he looked at her.

Kari didn't say another word. She'd said what she had to say.

But Alex had plenty to say. "Are you giving me an ultimatum? After all we've been through, you're giving me an ultimatum when you know I do not answer to ultimatums?"

Kari knew she was playing with fire. But Alex and his neglect had been playing with it too. Now somebody's shit was going to burn. Although inwardly and deep down, Kari had a sickening feeling it was going to be hers.

But she held to her guns. She didn't back down.

And Alex's heart didn't stop hammering. Because he knew, too, that they were at a crossroads. A dangerous crossroads.

They rode the rest of the way to the airfield in silence.

But when they got there, and Alex removed his hand from Kari's hand, and his bodyguard opened the back passenger car door for him, a kind of desperation came over Kari. How could she even think about leaving Alex? He was the best thing that had ever happened to her. What was her problem? And suddenly she felt a need to take it all back. She hated that she felt that way. Why did she suddenly feel so needy and clingy? But that was how she felt. And she couldn't deny it. She loved him too much!

She grabbed onto Alex's suit coat sleeve and leaned against him. "I don't want you to go," she said to him in tears.

Alex couldn't look at her. Because he knew, had he looked, he would have caved. But he couldn't cave. She knew he didn't play to ultimatums, yet she gave him one anyway? He told her he could lose his entire conglomerate if he didn't get that merger done. A conglomerate she knew took him a lifetime to build. A conglomerate she knew he had every intentions of leaving to Jordan and Angie as their legacy. But even after he said it, she still wanted him to choose as if his business was equal to her, when she had to know it wasn't even in the same ballpark.

He steeled himself and then looked at her. She was wiping away her tears. It broke his heart. "You and the children mean more to me than anything in this world. I demonstrate that love every way I know how. It has been a terrible year, and I've been on the road more than is reasonable, I know that. But once I get this merger done---"

"Then there'll be another one that has to get done. And then another one. And then more after those ones, Alex. It never ends. Ever since I married you, it has never ended."

"My businesses are not equal to you, Karena. And you know that."

"Yes, I do know it. They aren't equal to me and I never said they were. They're above me, that's what I'm saying."

"That's bullshit!"

"You have placed your businesses above me and the children because you devote all of your time and attention to those businesses. You can call it bullshit all you want. I call it a fact!"

Alex looked away from her. His anger was trying to surface, but he kept it tamped down. Because it was Kari. His heartbeat! He looked at her once more. "What do you want from me? Do you want me to stop trying and just let my businesses fail?"

"You know I don't want that."

"Then you've got to let me go and salvage this. We'll be okay. I promise you. But you've got to let me go and take care of this."

Kari stared at Alex. He was behaving as if he had to have her permission to leave. As if the future of his empire was in her hands. That wasn't fair. She wasn't letting him put that rap on her.

But then Alex said something that nearly stopped her heartbeat. "Kari, *please*," he begged her.

He said please? She was stunned. How could she not support him now, after he said please?

But she knew she still couldn't back down. Because if she did, it would never, ever end. It would never, ever change.

She stared at Alex as he stared at her. Two stubborn titans trying to hold onto each other, but their own needs too. And Kari couldn't cave. Not again. Not this time. Not after she told him not to go, and he was going anyway. "Your plane is waiting," she said to him.

Her words tore through the core of Alex's being like a hacksaw. How could she be so cold? He just *begged* her to reason with him. He just cut out his heart and gave it to her for safe keeping, and she threw it down and trampled on it. That was how it felt to him. That was how she made him feel in that moment. After all he did for her!

And there it was. His hurt. His pain. His disappointment bubbling to the surface too. Kari used to always be the one he could count on to understand him, and to be there for him. But now she was deserting him too.

He got out of the limousine and made his way across the tarmac. He didn't look back.

Kari was hurt that he didn't give in, not even an inch. But it wasn't surprising at all. He never gave in. He never caved. She was the giver, she was the caver. She was the one who laid down all that she knew herself to be for all these years and hid in Alex's giant shadow.

She was done hiding.

"Take me home," she said to the driver, as she decisively and angrily wiped her tears away.

CHAPTER TWENTY-THREE

Ezekiel and Paige kept taking peeps at the boss as they rode from the airport in Budapest to Beverly Norgate's Hungarian mansion. He looked so distracted, and so filled with worry that he looked almost ill. They had to stop themselves on several occasions from asking if he was well. They'd never seen him so *not* himself. And he was about to negotiate with Bev Norgate?

"Sir, perhaps we should go over the fine points again," said Ezekiel, his chief negotiator.

But Alex waved even the hint of anymore discussions away. Ezekiel and Paige looked at each other. But they were powerless.

The limousine entered the gates of Bev Norgate's mansion and stopped at the entrance doors. The negotiators were about to get out of the limo too, but when the door to the rented limousine was opened by Alex's bodyguard, Alex stopped them. "Wait here," he said as he got out alone. He knew how Bev negotiated. He knew she would not appreciate prying eyes. He buttoned his suitcoat, braced himself, and headed toward the entrance.

He entered the home and was escorted

to the parlor. It took nearly ten minutes but Bev eventually came in, fully clothed, which wasn't her usual negotiating style. She sat in the chair beside him.

"I knew you'd come here," she said. "Don't I look smashing? I have an engagement."

"Getting married?" Alex said with a smile.

"Not that kind!" Bev was firm. "Are you jetlagged? You are normally in your morning time in Florida. We are in our nighttime. I never could get used to the difference."

"Do we have a deal, Bev?" Alex wasn't interested in her commentary and she knew it.

"We have a deal," Bev said, "if you are willing to hold to your end of the bargain."

"That's a no. This merger is good for both companies and you know it. The terms are favorable for both of us."

"You come all this way to tell me what I already know? I am not renegotiating the terms of the deal. I agree that they are decent terms. Good for my company. Great for yours." She gave Alex a *don't try to shit on my head* look.

"What I am negotiating," said Bev, "is what you need to do to get me to yes. And I have already told you what you need to do. We can do it now. Right upstairs. Nobody but the two of us will ever know. And then I will sign that final document that puts us over the top. I will go to my engagement, and you can go back to America with a lifeline for your corporation to survive another day. One hour of your time, maybe even less than that if you're no longer as good as you used to be, and it's a yes. You refuse to give me that hour, then it is a no. A hard no," she added.

Alex sat there staring at Bev, but she wasn't even on his radar. He was thinking, and had been thinking nonstop, about Kari. She was the very essence of him. She meant everything in this world to him. Then why did he come all this way? Especially when he knew what Bev was asking of him. Why didn't he just let it all go and Bev and her sexual appetite be damned? Why was he so damned stubborn?

The writing had been on the wall a long time ago. But it was in that moment, as he sat in that Hungarian parlor looking at a very beautiful and desirable woman, did it become clear to him. Kari was right. He had to choose. There was no way he could continue to take his family through these ups and downs of the world of high finance and expect them to stay onboard for the ride. Even rollercoasters got old after the thousandth ride.

"What happened, Bev?" he asked her.

Bev looked curiously at him. "What on

earth are you talking about?"

"You used to be so unique."

"I am unique."

"Not pulling this shit, you aren't. This isn't uniqueness. This is desperation. This is loneliness. This is an aging woman reaching for a youth that long since left her. And she wants it back. We're not those two people anymore, Bev. And we will never be those two people again."

Bev just sat there. But her legendary unpredictability took over and she stood up and began removing every stitch of clothing she had on. "I want what I want. You want my signature. I want you. I have always wanted you and you know that. And if you truly need this signature, and you do, I will get what I want." Her panties, the last item she removed, was tossed at Alex.

Alex didn't bother catching it. It dropped at his shoe. He stood on his feet, trampling it. "The deal is the deal that's already on paper. That's it. That's all. I can guarantee you that your company will come out the better for making this deal. Given the parameters, it's the only deal you'll ever get to take your company to the highest level. I will do all I can to shepherd it through. But that's all you're getting from me."

"Not your body? Not even for an hour?"

"Not even for a second," Alex said.

That hurt Bev to her core. "Why are you doing this to me, Alexio?"

"Because I'm married," he said firmly. "I have a wife whom I love more than life itself. I have children. *A family*. I will not dishonor my wife."

Bev stared at him. That was why she wanted him. He was the only man she'd ever known with true morals. He was the only man that didn't treat her like a dog.

But nobody crossed Bev Norgate. "Then it's a no," she said.

Alex was disappointed. He needed her and she knew it. But he didn't delay. He left her parlor and began heading out of her home.

But just as he was nearing her front door and her butler was about to open it, he heard her voice.

"Alexio."

Alex stopped. Then he turned. Bev, still stark naked even though her butler was present, walked slowly toward him, with a folder in her hand. She handed it to Alex.

Alex opened it and looked at it. It was the final page of their merger deal, signed by Bev. He looked at her.

"I am putting my entire fortune into your hands. I had to make sure you were still a man of integrity and wouldn't screw me over." She smiled. "You passed the test," she said.

Alex stared at her. Who was she to test him? And somehow her yes meant about the same to him as her no. It was just a word.

But a needful word.

"Thank you," he said without adding any gratitude to such an insult when all she had to do was give him that signature while they were still in New York. And then he left her home.

But just as he was walking toward his limo, he stopped in his tracks. And then he frowned. And he remembered her words: *I knew you'd come here*, she had said to him. And he knew instantaneously something wasn't right.

He kept walking to his limo. As his bodyguard opened the door, he looked at him. "Get my brother on the phone," he said, and got inside.

CHAPTER TWENTY-FOUR

That next day, while Alex's private jet had entered U.S. airspace again after flying all night back from Hungary, Kari stared at the faces of the maid and the housekeeping supervisor as if she couldn't believe they would even attempt to justify what she'd uncovered. But that was exactly what they were doing.

"It wasn't like this," said the maid.

"Somebody had to have come back after she cleaned this room and did this," said her supervisor.

Kari was disgusted with both of them. The trash was swept into a pile and was not picked up. The countertops were filled with dust. The bathroom still reeked of beer and pot. "There was a party in this suite last night," Kari said. "After the guest checked out this morning, you came in here, cleaned it supposedly, and your supervisor gave it a clean bill. Which meant she reviewed your work and it passed inspection. The only inspection this shit would have passed is the inspection that never happened."

"But I did inspect this room," said the

supervisor. "But so what? This is no big deal. She missed a few places, that's all," she had the nerve to add.

Both Marcus McNeal, the hotel's security chief, and Deb Smith, Kari's assistant, who had come to the suite with her, were amazed by their willful ignorance. But the supervisor wouldn't let up. "It's just a little trash we missed. It's nothing I tell you."

"Perhaps it's nothing at the local hooker motel," said Kari. "But here, at The Drakos, it is not allowed! And this filth and smells aren't even the worst of it," she added as she walked over to the unmade bed. They all followed her.

"See," said the supervisor excitedly. "That bed was made up."

"That bed was made up," the maid agreed happily. "I told you somebody came back in here. That bed was made up!"

"I know it was," said Kari. "But you never changed the bedding like you know you must do after every single guest leaves. When my assistant reported back to me about the trash and filth she encountered on a random check of some of the rooms, I came up here and did my own inspection. I unmade that bed you so proudly made up. And this is what I found," Kari said as she pulled the top sheet all the way back. The fitted sheet was covered in various colors of vomit. So much so that even the maid and supervisor stepped back appalled.

"You didn't do a *got*damn thing to this suite," said Kari angrily. "Those idiots who stayed here last night made up the bed, and your ass glanced in, saw the bed made up, and hurried on to your next room." It took all Kari had to contain her rage. "But that is not allowed. Not in my hotel!" she declared.

"Don't you mean your husband's hotel?" the supervisor had the nerve to ask. "Last I looked a white man owns this hotel. We whites own this hotel," she said proudly. "You're just the help!"

Marcus and Deb glanced at each other and shook their heads. Kari stared at the supervisor, amazed too. Because Kari knew the deal. This woman, who worked for Kari, actually thought she was the superior being in that room because of her skin tone. But lest she forget. "You're fired," Kari said.

The supervisor and the maid were the only two people in that suite surprised by Kari's decision. The supervisor was floored. "Fired?" she asked. "Over *this*?"

"Both of you are fired," Kari made herself clear. Then she looked at Marcus. "Escort these two women off of this property immediately, and then notify HR."

"Yes, ma'am," Marcus said. "Let's go Thelma and Louise," he said to the two employees.

Kari looked at both of them. "Not bad, hun," she said, "for the help?" Then she gave both ladies another harsh look, and watched Marcus remove them from the suite. Then she ordered Deb to get another cleaning crew up here fast. And then Kari left the suite too.

Once she closed the door out in the hall, she leaned against it, still holding the knob. For the last few years she had been hoping to step back from oversight of the housekeeping department, simply because of the volume of work it entailed, but she realized once again that that wasn't going to happen. Pristine rooms were the most important function of a hotel. Period. A room out of order was a guest out of order, especially with the prices The Drakos were able to command. And had a guest seen the condition of that room, that filth, it would have been a catastrophic failure. And those buffoons thought it was no big deal? She shook her head. Then she pulled out her phone and glanced at her text messages again. Nothing from Alex again. Even after the way they parted.

"Ma! Ma! There you are!"

It was Jordan, who had just gotten off the elevator and was hurrying toward her, pushing up the glasses on his face as he did. She smiled and pushed away from the door when she saw her handsome son. She began walking toward him.

"I'm glad I found you."

"I didn't know I was lost."

"You have to call Dean Hurston," said Jordan as he began following his mother to the elevator. Dean Hurston was the dean at Angela's country day school.

"Why would I need to call Dean Hurston?"

"Angie's field trip to Disney is Saturday and Dad forgot to call him."

"But I thought he signed that field trip slip a month ago."

"He did. But the school says they must speak directly with each parent to ensure the students didn't forge their parents' names. They got sued apparently over that very thing and so they instituted this new policy that Dad knew about. Will you call him? I called on her behalf but they said it has to be a parent."

Jordan was like Angie's second daddy, rather than her big brother, but she understood the school couldn't see it that way. "Stop worrying, J. I'll call him the dean soon as I get back to my office."

Jordan exhaled. "Thanks, Ma," he said

as they made their way to the elevators. "She's looking forward to the trip and I don't want any last-minute hiccups."

"Yes, sir, boss," said Kari, and Jordan smiled.

The elevator doors opened and a cleaning crew stepped off. "Ma'am," said the head cleaner as they hurried to the unsanitary suite Kari had just left. She and Jordan stepped onto the elevator and began making their way downstairs.

Kari glanced at her phone again as a new text came in.

"Dad?" asked Jordan.

"Nope," said Kari, who didn't bother to read the text when she saw who it wasn't from.

"What husband and father goes all the way to Hungary and not bother to check on his own family?"

"He knows his brother is here and will let him know if anything's wrong."

"But that's not the point," said Jordan. "Don't make excuses for him."

"What excuse? I was just telling you how he's probably thinking."

The elevator door opened on the second floor, where Kari was heading. "I love him, too, Ma," Jordan said as Kari stepped off. "But don't make excuses for him. He'll never learn if we keep excusing him." The elevator doors closed again to take Jordan back downstairs.

Kari just stood there. Was that what she was doing? Something she swore she'd never do? But she knew what she was up against. All those females out there wanting to wrangle themselves a great looking guy like Alex, and a billionaire to boot? And the greatest guy she'd ever known? And his devotion to his conglomerate? She knew what she was up against.

She began walking back toward her office when her emergency button sounded. She quickly looked at her phone and saw that the emergency was in suite 652, which was the very floor she was on. She phoned for Marcus to meet her at that room as she hurried to the suite.

When she got there, she knocked. When she got no response, she quickly used her master keycard to swipe the lock and enter the suite. But when she heard a woman's voice crying, she slowly walked toward the bedroom. But when the woman cried *Don't kill me! Please don't stab me with that knife*! she knew she had no time to waste.

She pulled out the fully-loaded Glock she kept zipped in her coat pocket, a necessity ever since she married Alex Drakos, and she hurried toward the bedroom sounds.

When she stepped in with both hands on her gun, and her gun aimed, she yelled herself. "Drop that knife now! Drop it!"

The man, who was naked and on top of one of Kari's maids, seemed to not even hear her. He lifted his hand and was about to stab the maid when Kari knew she had no choice. She fired one shot into his back. The assailant dropped the knife and the maid jumped out of bed away from him as he laid there unconscious.

"Are you okay?" Kari asked anxiously asked the maid.

The maid could only muster a nod.

Kari quickly got on her walkie talkie and told Marcus to come now. Shots had been fired.

Kari, shaken herself, hurried over to the man and checked his pulse. But it only confirmed what she suspected all along. He was gone. Her maid was spared from what appeared to be certain death. But her assailant was in fact dead. And Kari could hardly believe it.

Stunned by the sudden turn of events, and the maid shaking worse than Kari was, she personally called 911. She thought she was going to join that rapist the way her heart was pounding. But she kept it together. For her maid's sake, she didn't fall to pieces too.

CHAPTER TWENTY-FIVE

The detective pushed off from the wall outside of suite 652 when two additional detectives, including the lead detective from Robbery/Homicide, got off the elevator and made their way to where he was standing.

"Heads up," he said.

"Don't tell me it's another athlete," said the lead detective. "I hate dealing with those entitled idiots."

"No athlete," said the waiting detective.

"Then what's the heads up?"

"The perp? The shooter? It's Alex Drakos's wife."

Both detectives were astonished. "Shit," said the second detective.

"Are you certain?" asked the lead detective.

"Positive. We didn't put it over the radio or mention it to anybody because Brass don't want the press all over it yet. But yeah, it's the big man's wife."

The lead detective smiled and rubbed his forehead. "Shit like this," he said, "can make a career. Or ruin it," he added, and then exhaled. "Where is she?"

173

"We put her in an unoccupied suite across the hall from the crime scene. She's acting like it's no big deal. But it is," he added and handed the lead detective his notes.

When the lead read the notes, he looked at his subordinate with shock in his eyes. "I'll be damn," he said.

"What is it?" asked his number two.

The lead handed the notes to his number two and then walked over to the suite across the hall. The number two, on seeing what surprised his colleague, hurried behind him, shocked too.

But as soon as they entered the room, they dismissed the lone uniformed officer standing guard. Kari, along with Marcus McNeal, were seated on the sofa. The lead detective sat in the chair. "Hello, Mrs. Drakos."

"I don't mean to be rude," said Kari, "but I have a hotel to run. I gave the other officer my statement. I don't understand why that isn't enough. I'm sorry it happened. I truly didn't want it to happen. But he left me no choice."

"Why did you shoot him?" asked the lead detective.

Kari looked at him. "I told the other detective already. He wrote it down."

"Tell it to me."

Kari exhaled. She was still shaken by it all, even though she was trying with all she had not to show it. "I walked into the suite."

"Your husband owns the hotel. You're the most senior member of this organization after him. Why would you need to be in that suite?"

"Because I run the operations of this hotel. And I received a distress beep coming from suite 652. Our maids keep a panic button in their pockets. When I walked in, I saw the man attempting to rape my maid, and was about to stab her."

"So you just shot him?"

"I warned him first, and then I fired one shot, yes. He was going to kill my maid. His hand was lifted, ready to stab her. There was no time to waste. He was going to kill her."

"According to whom?"

Kari looked at the detective. "According to the knife he had in his hand lifted and ready to stab."

"The maid said she was cleaning the room when you came through that door yelling at the guest. She assumed you knew him and he had broken your heart or something romantic had gone on between the two of you."

Kari frowned. "*What*?"

Even her security chief looked at the detective astonished. "What are you talking about?" Marcus asked him.

But the detective ignored him. "Are you saying right now that you didn't know him, Mrs. Drakos?" the detective asked Kari.

"Yes, that's exactly what I'm saying. I didn't know him at all!"

"Your maid said it was a heated exchange, as if you knew him, and then your bad temper took over and you shot him in cold blood."

Kari could not believe her ears. "He was naked on top of her!"

"She said he was naked in his own bed, and was under the covers the entire time she was there."

"But he had a knife," said Marcus. "What about the knife?"

"We didn't find any knife in that room. Or in that entire suite," said the detective. "No knife has been recovered anywhere."

Kari was blown away with amazement. She knew she saw a knife. She was certain she saw that knife!

The detective looked at Marcus. "Did you see a knife?"

"I wasn't looking for one. I never searched the room. It was a crime scene. But if Mrs. Drakos says she saw a knife, she saw a knife."

"Nobody else saw one, not even the

maid," said the detective, and everybody looked at Kari.

Kari knew she was in the kind of trouble that could be her ultimate undoing. The maid lying? No knife? A man dead? *"What the fuck,"* she said out loud.

The detective rose to his feet and nodded toward the two uniform officers in the room. "Mrs. Karena Drakos you are hereby under arrest for the murder of Joe Colburn. You have the right to remain silent. Anything you say can and will be used against you in a court of law." He began her Miranda warnings as the other detective cuffed and frisked her.

"I'll call the attorneys," said Marcus nervously. He could only imagine how angry the boss was going to be.

But Kari saying no as the detective began taking her out of the suite. "You call my husband, and then notify Oz. I'm being railroaded. Those attorneys can't do shit for me. I'm being framed," she cried out, as they carted her away.

CHAPTER TWENTY-SIX

Alex got off of his plane and hurried up to the SUV waiting at the foot of the stairs. The bodyguard opened the door as Alex hopped in. Oz was on the backseat, and the bodyguard hopped back onto the front seat as the SUV sped away.

"What do we know so far?" Alex asked anxiously. He still couldn't believe it.

"They took her into custody."

"I know they took her into custody, Oz. But has she bailed out yet?"

"Not yet. They haven't even had her bond hearing yet. At least that's what the lawyers are telling me."

"But murder? They got her on a murder rap? How in hell could that happen?"

"I haven't heard the story from her, but according to our sources at the police department she claimed one of our maids were being raped by one of our guests, she happened upon the scene somehow, and she shot and killed the perp in defense of her maid."

"Then why did they arrest her?"

"The maid doesn't corroborate the story. She said the man was flirtatious, and they were playing around, but he never had a knife and he never threatened her."

Alex was confused. "But surely they recovered the knife at the scene. Right?"

Oz exhaled. "Wrong."

Alex was floored. "What do you mean wrong? There was no knife?"

"According to our sources, and I was just able a few minutes ago to get him on the phone, he said they didn't find any knife in that suite whatsoever. Not even a pocket knife. Not any weapon at all."

Alex leaned his head back. "No wonder they're slow-walking bail. They got themselves a Drakos and they aim to keep her."

"It's a lot," said Oz. "It's a lot."

"Can't you go faster than this?" Alex barked at his driver. "Get me to that police station and get me there faster than this!"

"Yes, sir," the driver said, and sped up even more.

Alex looked at Oz. "I thought you were still in Philly. You were in Philly when I called you about Bev approving the deal."

"I flew right back when Marcus called me about Kari."

"I told you to be in town when I'm out of town," said Alex.

"I was gone before you left town. How

was I to know you'd wake up and suddenly had to go right back off again?"

Alex knew that was another issue that he couldn't deal with right now.

"And we didn't find a connection, in case you're wondering."

Alex looked at his kid brother. "What?"

"When you called me from Hungary and asked me to see if there was a connection between Southeast and Bev? We haven't found one so far."

"Keep looking."

"But why would you think there would be a connection?"

"When Bev left New York and went back to Budapest, and I showed up, she said she knew I'd come."

"Because we have to have that merger," said Oz. "Makes sense."

"But it didn't feel like that. It felt like . . ."

Oz looked at his brother. He respected his instincts as if they were gospel. "Like what, Alexio? What did it feel like?"

"Like a distraction. Like they needed me out of town. Like they . . ." Then as soon as Alex said those words, it came to him.

Oz saw the change on his face. "Tell me what you're thinking, brother. And who are they?"

"Like this whole thing is being orchestrated."

Oz turned toward his brother. "What whole thing? Kari's arrest?"

"Kari's arrest. That mass shooting. Diallo Koffi! Athens."

"What are you saying, brother?"

"Maybe it all was meant to be a big distraction."

"But what from?"

"I don't know," Alex said, but he was thinking hard. Then he looked at Oz. "I want you to send a plane to Greece, along with our top security team, and escort every member of my board of directors in my southeast sector here."

"Here? Bring them here to Florida?"

"Bring them here. Bring every one of those motherfuckers to me."

But Oz was baffled. "Let me get this straight. You think those missing funds from Dave Pantanzis and your southeast board, and the assassination of Walter Vokos, has something to do with Kari's arrest?"

"And all the rest of it too, yes," said Alex.

"But how? But why?"

"I don't know how or why! But every fiber of my being is telling me it all connects. Somehow it all connects, Odysseus."

Oz had never seen Alex look more certain. He pulled out his phone to notify his pilot. "I'll make it happen," he said.

Alex thought about his wife in some filthy jail, and his heart was racing again. "Can you go any faster?" he yelled at his driver.

CHAPTER TWENTY-SEVEN

Before the SUV could come to a complete stop, Alex was opening the back door and hurrying out. Oz jumped out with him and they both hurried up the steps of the AVPD. But to their surprise, Benny Church and a team of lawyers were just coming out.

"She's still locked up, Ben?" asked Alex as he and the lawyers met midway on the steps.

"She made bail," said Benny.

"So she's out?"

"She's out, yes, sir."

"Then where is she?" Alex asked, looking around.

"We don't know where she's at, sir," said another one of the attorneys.

Alex and Oz both looked at the attorney. "What's that supposed to mean?"

The attorney looked at Benny. Although he wasn't senior attorney on the case, he had more clout because of his friendship with the boss. "She was bailed out," Benny said, "but not by us."

"Then who bailed her out?"

"A Mr. Diallo Koffi," said Benny.

"Koffi? What does he have to do with my

wife?"

"We got word that bail had been set when we didn't even know that a bail hearing had been scheduled, but we rushed over here anyway to pay whatever the bail was. But Mr. Koffi, apparently, did know about the bail hearing and he beat us to it. She left with him before we could get here."

"What about her security detail?" Alex asked, looking around. "Where the hell were they?"

"They thought she was still in jail. They left."

Alex was so angry he could hardly contain his fury. Oz immediately got on his phone. Alex immediately tried to phone Kari again. But it only rang and rang. He took off. Oz took off after him.

"She'd better not be with that bastard," Alex said as he ran, although his heart wasn't so defiant. His heart was praying that she wasn't with Diallo Koffi.

"Put Marcus on the phone," said Oz as they hopped back into the SUV. But this time Alex got behind the wheel, Oz got on the front passenger seat, and the bodyguard and driver got in the back.

"Marcus, have you seen Mrs. Drakos?" Then Oz looked at Alex. "You have?"

"Where is she?" Alex asked.

"Where is she?" Oz asked into the phone. Then he smiled. "Oh good!" He looked at Alex. "She's at the penthouse."

And Alex exhaled. "At least that!" he said. And then he made a quick U-turn and headed to The Drakos instead of Diallo's mansion.

But Alex's anger was still there. And he hit the steering wheel repeatedly. "How the fuck could you let this happen?" he asked his brother as Oz ended the call.

Oz looked at Alex. "Me?"

"How could you drop the ball like this, Odysseus? You should have been here!"

"Well excuse me for being in Philly with my family. Had I known she would shoot somebody and get herself arrested, then I would have been here. I would have made it my business to be here and you know it! And you have the nerve to say I should have been here? What about you? Your ass should have been here!"

Alex kept on driving. Because he knew Oz was right. He could blame it on the moon, sun, and stars, but that still wasn't going to exonerate him.

"Come on!" he said when cars backed up at a red light forced him to stop too. The tension, the anxiety, the guilt all over his body was as clear as his red knuckles gripping the steering wheel.

CHAPTER TWENTY-EIGHT

Kari leaned her head back in the tub and took another sip of wine. She was glad to be back home, but it seemed so temporary. Because she still had those charges over her head. She still was thrown into a jail cell like a common prisoner with everybody gawking at her as the wife of a billionaire. It was awful.

She still recalled the relief she felt the moment they came to that filthy cell and said she could go. That she had been bailed out. She expected to see Alex standing there. Or at least Oz or Benny or somebody from their team. But it was Diallo. It was disconcerting that Alex wasn't there, but she was grateful to have Diallo.

But she also remembered when she got in his car and realized they weren't headed in the right direction.

"Take me home," she said to him. "What are you doing?" Didn't he realize how badly she just wanted to go home?

"The press may be at The Drakos awaiting your arrival," Diallo said. "You will stay with me until they leave."

"No, I won't either. Take me home, Dee. I'm going home."

"Is that any kind of way to speak to the man who bailed you out?"

Kari looked at him. "Nobody told your ass to bail me out. For real. I could have bailed my own ass out, and I would have arranged it. But you did it without me even having a bail hearing. I didn't know it worked that way."

"Money talks. Unlike your husband, I'm willing to spend mine on a worthy cause."

"I'll pay you back every dime. Just take me home."

Diallo looked puzzled. "Why are you upset with me, Karena? What have I done to you except give you a great investment opportunity? Except help you every chance I can?"

Kari wasn't trying to hear any of it. After the way he showed his behind with Alex in that diner put the brakes on their partnership. Nobody was disrespecting her husband. "Take me home, Dee," she said again.

"You will stay with me," he said again.

Kari quickly opened the car door. "I'll jump out of this motherfucker. Take me home!"

"Okay, okay," said Diallo nervously. He realized he didn't know her well enough to know if she was bluffing or dead serious. By her demeanor, he called it serious. "I shall take you home. Close the door."

Kari hesitated, and then she closed the door.

Now she was home and Diallo was gone. Something about him rubbed her wrong at that diner. It was as if she saw a side of him that she didn't like at all. But she couldn't put her finger on what it was. But it was there. And the fact that she had to threaten to jump out of his car to get him to take her home just pissed her off. Who did he think he was? Didn't he realize she was so terrified of what could happen to her in the criminal justice system that her entire body was shaking? She pulled out her hand to see if her nerves had calmed. But they had not. Her hand was still trembling. And Diallo didn't give a shit.

But then she forgot about Diallo when she heard Alex's voice.

"Kari? Kari?"

She could hear him running up the stairs.

"Karena?"

When he made it upstairs and saw that she wasn't in the bedroom, he hurried into the ensuite. When he saw her in their tub, and was all in one piece, he leaned against the doorjamb relieved. Then he walked further into the massive bathroom and sat in one of the two high-back resting chairs.

They said nothing to each other. Mainly

because neither one of them knew where to even begin.

Kari took a few more sips of her wine, and then stood up to get out of the tub.

As she stepped out, Alex grabbed a big towel from the rack, walked up to her, and began drying her off. Kari stood there and allowed it, because she knew how much she needed Alex. She talked her shit to him, and he talked his shit to her, but they were always the ones they turned to when they needed help the most.

When Alex finished drying her off, he lifted her into his arms. She needed that too. She wrapped her legs around him and laid her head on his shoulder as he carried her to their bedroom. When he put her in bed, she turned onto her side and watched as he laid on top of the covers beside her, fully dressed in his business suit, and turned onto his side as well.

And for several moments they just laid there, staring at each other.

And then Kari spoke. "I'm scared, Alex."

Alex's heart dropped when she said those words. He placed his hand on the side of her face. But he wasn't there to talk. He was there to listen.

"They set me up. I got a distress call that there was trouble in 652. I was already on the floor so I hurried over to the suite. I knocked, but nobody answered. So I walked on in. And when I heard my maid telling the guy to stop hurting her, and to not kill her and she mentioned a knife, I eased to the bedroom. But when I saw him on top of my maid with a knife in his hand ready to stab her, I had to act. I had to do something or he was going to kill her. So I pulled out my Glock and did something. I saw him with my own two eyes, Alex. He had a knife and he was about to stab my maid to death. But now she claims I'm lying. She's trying to say I was having an affair with the guy or some other nonsense. And they haven't found any knife in that suite."

"What's the maid's name?"

"Sabrina Crosby."

"And the guest?"

"They said his name, but I don't remember it."

Alex nodded. "I'll look into it." He rubbed her face. "I'll take care of you."

Kari stared into his eyes. "Will you?"

It broke Alex's heart. But he understood her doubts. "Yes. I will."

"You left when I asked you to stay."

Alex frowned and nodded. "Yes, I did that too." He fought back tears. "I'm sorry I did that." He looked into her eyes. "I am so sorry."

Kari continued to stare at him. He was

hurting too. "Do we have a merger?"

Alex was embarrassed to even admit it. But he nodded his head.

Kari exhaled. "Good. I would have kicked your ass had you left me and came back emptyhanded."

Alex smiled. That was the old Kari he knew!

But then their smiles slowly faded, and the reality that Kari was still in trouble crystallized, and Alex pulled her into his arms.

Late that afternoon, Oz walked into the penthouse as Alex, with a folder in his hand, was coming out of his home office.

"You rang, brother?"

"I need you to stay here with Karena."

"Where are the kids?"

"They're on their way home with tight security. I sent Tope to supervise. I wanted to wait until the end of the school day since Jordan had a midterm in his last class."

"Good," said Oz, who was closer to Jordan than any family member. "He worries too much anyway. What about Kari? What's she up to?"

"She's asleep. And let her sleep. She needs it." Alex began heading for the exit. "I've got to make a run."

Oz was floored. "A run? You're kidding me. *Now*?"

"I'll be back," Alex said, and left without explanation.

Oz shook his head. That boneheaded brother of his would never change! But it wasn't as if he could judge. His family was in Philly with his father-in-law. And even when he went there, to bring them back home, it didn't go well. Who was he to talk? He and his brother, he knew deep down as he made his way into the living room, weren't all that dissimilar.

CHAPTER TWENTY-NINE

"Uncle Oz, is it true?"

Jordan was behind the wheel of his Chevy Camaro driving himself and his sister home from school. Two different security cars, one in front of Jordan and one behind him, were escorting them in. But Aaron "Tope" Toparta, the chief of the family's security details, had already told Jordan that his mother had been arrested and he needed to go straight home without making any of the various stops he usually made along the way. But as Jordan drove, stunned by the news, he phoned his uncle for confirmation.

But Oz, on the other end of the call, was being coy. "Is what true?"

"About Ma! Tope said she was *arrested*?"

Angela looked over at Jordan.

"When did he tell you that?"

"Unc, is it true? What difference does it make when he told me? Just tell me if it's true or not!"

There was a pause. "Yes," he said. "It's true. But she's okay. She's home. It's just a bunch of b.s. You just come on home, alright?"

"Can I talk to her?"

"No. She's sleeping, and your father doesn't want anybody disturbing her. Just come on home."

Jordan exhaled. "Okay," he said, and ended the call.

"Mommy's rested?"

Jordan almost corrected his baby sister, and then realized it was best she thought what she thought. "Yep, she's resting. She's sleeping."

"Why did you need to know if it was true that she was rested?"

"Because I wanted to know. Is that a crime all of a sudden? Stop asking so many questions."

"You like when I ask questions. You said I'm smart to ask a lot of questions."

"Not today, Ang, okay? Not today," added Jordan as he gripped the steering wheel while passing by a BP gas station.

But just as he was about to pass on by, a pickup truck came speeding out of that gas station parking lot and pulled out just in front of him.

"*Ah man!*" Jordan yelled out as he was forced to take his steering wheel and swerve violently to avoid hitting the pickup. But he sideswiped the truck anyway, forcing his car to lean on two wheels. Jordan, not an experienced driver at all, overcorrected the wrong way and his car, with him and his baby sister inside, began flipping across lanes, frontend to backend, like an out-of-control pogo stick. It was flipping repeatedly, and so out-of-control that another car, in a different lane, tried to swerve out of its way but ended up hitting it too. Another truck hit them too.

By the time Jordan's Camaro came to a final stop, it was spinning upside down and so mangled and crushed that it was unrecognizable. The security team, mortified, hopped out of their cars and ran to the aid of the Drakos children as fast as they could. They couldn't get there fast enough.

"Call 911," Tope was yelling as he beat all of Security running to that car. This was on his watch. This was at his feet.

"Lord have mercy," Tope cried. "Call 911!"

CHAPTER THIRTY

The SUV sped up to the hospital entrance and Tope, waiting outside, opened the back passenger door.

"Where are they?" Kari asked as she jumped out, along with Oz, and they all began running into the hospital.

"Jordan's okay," said Tope. "He's banged up, but he's okay."

"And Angie?"

Tope hesitated. Which caused Kari and Oz to both stop in their tracks.

"What about my baby?" asked a terrified Kari.

"Mrs. Drakos."

They all looked around and saw a somber-looking doctor walking toward them. "Hello ma'am."

"Where's my daughter? What's happened to my daughter?"

The doctor seemed as hesitant as Tope. But he spoke. "She's in surgery, ma'am."

197

"Surgery?" Kari was certain she'd heard him wrong. "My baby's in *surgery*?"

"I'm afraid so, yes, ma'am. We were concerned that there may be some internal bleeding. We had to act and act immediately."

"*Internal bleeding*?" Kari thought she was having a heart attack. "Oh my God!"

"Come and have a seat, ma'am please," the doctor said as Oz grabbed hold of Kari too. But he was in no shape either. He thought he was about to have a heart attack too.

But Kari jerked away from him and the doctor. "I want to see my son. Take me to my son."

"Perhaps you would prefer to sit first," the doctor said, but Kari wasn't trying to hear that.

"Take me to my son!" And her tone said it all. It wasn't a request, but an order.

"Yes, ma'am," the doctor said, obeying the order, as he escorted them to the elevators.

CHAPTER THIRTY-ONE

Catherine "Cate" Drakos strapped Jovani into her car seat on the backseat of her Porsche Panamera, put on her shades, and then got in behind the wheel. Now that she was no longer in her father's crosshairs, and was receiving a twenty-thousand-dollar monthly allowance from him, life was good. She knew she was getting the money mainly to take care of his beloved granddaughter, but at least she was getting it. She felt as if she was finally getting somewhere.

She looked through her rearview at Jovani. "Ready to go shopping, Baby Girl?"

Her little girl could only flap her legs and clap her hands, but it was enough for Cate. She laughed and pulled out of the driveway of her two-story condo on Pensacola Beach: another gift from her father. Her security detail, hired by her father as well, pulled out behind her.

But they weren't two blocks from her

home when the sound of gunfire could suddenly be heard. Cate looked out of her rearview and could see her security detail suddenly skirt out from behind her car and attempt to move beside it to protect Cate and the baby. But the driver of the detail car was hit by what seemed like sniper fire from a distance and the car lost control, veering away from Cate's Porsche.

Cate tried to speed up, to get away from the gunfire herself, but her front windshield was shot out and shattered, causing her to cover her face from the flying glass and to lose control of her vehicle too. As the detail car was hit again and exploded into a fireball, Cate's car lost traction and sailed across the sidewalk like a speedboat. It would have kept on sailing, and Cate would have kept on screaming, had it not crashed into a cement pole.

Her airbags deployed and other people nearby ran to her and her security detail's aid.

But Cate was more concerned for her child. "Are you okay, Jo-Jo?" she was asking frantically as she jerked off her seatbelt and crawled into the backseat to her baby. Jovani, like Cate, was okay too.

She pulled Jovani out of the car seat and held her tightly, tears streaming down her eyes.

She looked over at her the car driven by her security team and saw that none of the men were able to get out of that car before it exploded. Not one of them survived. And had the sniper fire ended? She got down on the floor of her car, crying and holding her crying baby even tighter.

CHAPTER THIRTY-TWO

"The Governor will see you now, sir."

Alex stood up and walked down the long corridor to the office of the Governor of Florida. Mel Chudney, the governor, stood up from his desk with a grand smile and an extended hand.

"Alex Drakos! It's been a month of Sundays since I saw you last. Been out on the links lately? Still shaming your golf partners?"

"I do my best," Alex said as he and the governor shook hands. "How have you been, Mel?"

"Terrible. Upset stomach all the time. They got a name for it. IBD or IBF or some such fancy-dancy name. I hate it! Sit down."

Alex sat in front of the desk and the governor sat back down. "So what do I owe this honor? Planning to open another hotel? Another casino? The answer is yes! You're good for business."

"My wife is in trouble," Alex said.

The governor continued to smile, but it slowly faded. "Oh *that*," he said. "But you know how that goes. It's not like I didn't warn you."

Alex frowned. "Didn't warn me about what?"

"Marrying that gal. When you first decided to invest in Florida, I wasn't governor then, but I was in the state House and attended several dinners in your honor. And I told you then it was a bad idea. I figure people should marry within their stations in life. You been rich your whole life. That gal was a maid!"

She actually owned her own cleaning service, but whether she was rich or poor was beside the point to Alex. He hated those obnoxious politicians. But for Kari's sake, he held his fire.

"I'm shocked it hasn't hit the airways yet. But it's all been under the radar. Which is good. Bad press in a tourist town is bad all around."

"A couple news outlets got wind of it," said Alex, "but my people were able to get them to put a lid on it for twenty-four hours."

"Why? What difference will twenty-four hours make?"

"Enough time for me to come see you. Enough time for you to work your magic."

The governor smiled again, but he was already shaking his head. "I can't work no magic in that case. Now you know I'll do anything for you. You're a valued member of my state. The richest member of my state," he added with a chuckle, "and we got some rich bastards in this state. But that wife of yours is accused of murder, Alex. Not speeding. Not driving drunk even. Murder. She killed a man. Some say it was her lover, and I don't have cause to doubt that. What the fuck I'm gonna do with a hot potato like that?"

"You're going to contact your Attorney General, who will in turn contact the state attorney for my county, who will in turn notify police that all charges are dropped against my wife. That's what you'll do."

The governor looked at Alex as if he'd grown a third eye. "You must be insane! Why on earth would I risk my entire political future on getting caught up in a murder investigation?"

Alex leaned forward. "You will risk it," he said, "or you will have no political future."

The governor frowned. "What are you threatening me? Is that Greek mafia shit resurfacing again? The FBI knows all about your past, and your brother's maybe not so past. Don't push it."

Alex took the folder he had brought with him and tossed it onto the governor's desk.

"What's this?"

Alex said nothing.

The governor took the folder and opened it. A series of pictures greeted him. All with the smiling faces of three different children. Three beautiful biracial children. The governor's jaw almost dropped. He looked up at Alex as if he was stunned. "How did you know . . . How could you know . . ."

"If charges are not dropped," Alex said, "your secret love children by your former housekeeper will be given to any news outlet that wants the story. Which, in Florida, will be all of them. Your wife would probably also want to know a little more about this very secret situation as well."

"You bastard!" the governor yelled with clenched teeth. "You bastard!"

Alex stood up. "Don't fuck with me, Mel, or I'll expose that little secret and a whole lot more before I'm done. My wife did not shoot that man for the hell of it. She shot him to prevent a murder. Those charges had better be dropped or you won't have to worry about a political future. You won't have to worry about a future at all. Get it done," Alex said with rage in his eyes.

Then he turned and left the office. The governor looked at those pictures again, pictures of his three out-of-wedlock children his wife knew nothing about. And he grabbed the folder and threw it across the room. "Bastard!" he yelled again.

Alex felt like a bastard, too, as he got into

his limo outside of the governor's mansion in Tallahassee and leaned his head back. He hated that underhanded shit more than the governor did.

But before he could get into the car, his security detail chief hurried up to him. "We just got the call, sir. They said they tried to phone you directly."

"I was meeting with the governor. No phones allowed. Why? What is it?"

"There's been a car crash. An awful crash, sir."

"Involving who?"

"Jordan, sir."

Alex was mortified. "Ah Jesus, no!"

"And little Angela too, sir."

Alex frowned. "What? They're okay, though. Tell me my children are okay!"

"Jordan is okay. But Angela's in surgery."

Alex's eyes stretched in horror and he jumped into his limo. The detail chief jumped in with him.

"Get me to the airport as fast as you can get me there," he ordered his driver, and the driver took off.

Alex thought he was going to die. In his wildest imaginings of his family in crisis, he had not imagined that all of them, all at once, would be in danger. He quickly phoned Kari's phone, but it rang and rang. He was about to phone Oz when his chief spoke again.

"There's more, sir," the chief said.

Alex looked at him. More? Was he out of his mind? How could there be more? Then he realized how, and his heart nearly stopped. "It's my wife?"

"No, sir."

"My brother?"

"No, sir, it wasn't either of them. But it does concern your daughter and your granddaughter."

"Please don't tell me my grandbaby was in an accident too."

"This was no accident, sir. There was a sniper."

Alex frowned. "A sniper?"

"Whomever it was, they fired from a distance and took out Cate's entire security detail, all of them are dead."

Alex was mystified. He had no words.

"And that sniper fire also struck Cate's vehicle and caused her to crash into a cement pole. But she and Jovani are absolutely okay."

Alex exhaled. At least that! But then he fell back against his seat as if the wind had been knocked out of him.

"What's happening, sir?" the detail chief asked. He was as bewildered as Alex.

But Alex was as clueless as he was. "Get me to the airport," he said again to his driver. But this time, he didn't realize, it didn't sound like a command. It was in a voice so weak with concern for his family that it was nothing more than a whisper.

CHAPTER THIRTY-THREE

They sat in Jordan's hospital suite awaiting a word, *any word*, from the surgeons. It had been hours, but all they knew was that Angela was still in surgery. Jordan had cuts and bruises and a broken arm, but Tope was right: he was banged up but okay. Every test they ran was negative on Jordan. It was Angie they were worried about.

But every time Jordan grimaced, Kari jumped up. "Are you in pain, son? You need me to call the nurse?"

"I'm okay," said Jordan. "It hurts a little, but I don't want any pain pills. I've got friends hooked on that stuff. I don't want that." Then he sighed. "I just want Angie to be okay."

Kari wanted it too. And she wasn't going to lie and pretend it wasn't bad. Even their family physician, who rushed over, said it was bad. She went to Jordan and put her arms around him and held him tightly.

Oz leaned back in his chair and stared at Kari. She was a strong woman who loved her family with an undying love. She could take the heat. But when word came that her children had been in a car crash, all she could think to do was grab a pair of jeans, an oversized jersey, and a pair of her Jordans, and take off. She put her hair up in a ponytail as she was running down the stairs. Oz was thrown when he saw her coming down. She looked so young, she looked like a teenager. But up close, she looked so worried she looked like she'd aged decades.

The door to Jordan's suite opened, and Tope peered inside. "We just got word from Philadelphia, sir, that your wife is on her way back to Apple Valley on her father's plane."

"Okay good," said Oz.

"With her father," said Tope.

Oz didn't expect to hear that. Kari and Jordan were surprised too. "With her father?" Oz asked.

"Yes, sir, that's our information."

"Okay, Tope, thanks."

Tope nodded, backed back out, and closed the door behind him.

Kari looked at Oz. "You knew he was coming?"

"No way."

"Why's he coming?" Jordan asked.

"He wants to make sure you and Angie are okay. He's my father-in-law. You guys are my niece and nephew. We're family."

"But he's so mean," said Jordan. "I don't think I've ever seen that man smile one time."

"Quit lying, boy."

"I'm serious! He's mean."

"He's the king of the hill," said Oz. "And don't you forget it."

But Kari had Angie on her mind. "Why is it taking so long?" she asked as she began pacing the floor.

And just like that, they settled back into quietness again.

And then less than a half hour later, a flustered Alex was walking through that door.

But as soon as Kari saw him, her rage unleashed. "Where were you?" she yelled. "Our daughter is in surgery and your ass wasn't here?"

But before Alex could say a word, she was taking off one of her shoes and throwing it at him. 'Get out!" she yelled, as her shoe missed. "Get out! I mean it, get out of here!" Then she rushed over to him and started beating on him with her fists.

"Ma stop!" Jordan was pleading with her.

Oz had to grab her, terrified like Jordan was that Alex was going to kick her ass. But Alex just took it.

"Get him out of here!" Kari was crying as Oz held her back. "Get him out of here!"

"Go in the hall, Alex," Oz urged his brother as he fought to hold Kari back.

Alex was devastated that he was missing in action when he was needed again. He looked over at Jordan, who was looking angrily at him too, and he did as Oz suggested and left the room.

When Kari settled back down, Oz released her and then went out into the hall with his brother. said to his brother as he hurriedly pushed him out of the hospital suite and into the hall outside Jordan's hospital suite where Tope and the two guards on post were standing. He closed the door behind him. "She's upset," Oz said.

"And I'm not?" Alex's voice spewed anger. "That's my baby in surgery too. Not just hers!"

"You could have phoned her, Alexio, what's wrong with you?"

"I did phone her. Several times. But she wouldn't answer. So I phoned you."

"But you still didn't tell me where you were."

"What the fuck difference does that make?" Alex was enraged. He wasn't about to discuss his trip to the governor's mansion in case it didn't materialize. "I'm here now. That's what counts." Then he ran his hands through his hair. "She's still in surgery?"

Oz nodded. "The last update we got was

that she was still under the knife."

"Sweet Jesus," said Alex with pure anguish in his voice. "My baby under the knife." He shook his head. Then he looked at Oz again. "And Jordan's okay?"

"He's okay. Banged up, but okay."

"Tope sent me pics of the wreckage. Did you see it?"

Oz nodded.

"It's a wonder anybody survived that crash."

"It was horrific, that was for sure," said Oz.

Alex exhaled and nodded. Just thinking about it made him nauseous. "And what about this sniper situation with Cate and Jovani?"

"Wiped out her entire detail."

"Yeah, I know. And the sniper, whomever it was, got away?"

"Yup," Oz said with a nod of his head. "Have you spoken to Cate?"

"I phoned her on the way back. She put Jo on video so I could see for myself that she was okay. She's fine."

"Good," said Oz, nodding. "That's good."

"I ordered tight security for her and Jo at her condo, sir," said Tope. "Three details are on patrol. Cate wanted to come here to the hospital, so she and the baby could be with the family, but I didn't think that was a good idea."

"It wasn't," said Oz. "You made the right call."

Alex started pacing the floor. He was trying to wrap his brain around what all was going on.

Oz was trying to do the same thing. "What in hell is going on, Alex?" he asked his big brother.

Alex shook his head. "I don't know," he said painfully. Then he looked at Tope. "Do we know who the driver that pulled out in front of Jordan was?"

"Yes, sir. It was Peter Saulsby. 59-year-old shoe salesman."

"Was it a hit-and-run?"

"No sir. He remained at the scene. He admitted his fault. He was booked in the county jail on failure to yield."

"*Failure to yield*? He nearly killed my children and they're calling it a *failure to yield*?!"

Then Alex just stood there, and tried to calm himself back down. "My baby is in surgery," he said to nobody in particular. "My son is in a hospital room. My grandbaby was nearly killed. And I wasn't there for any of them. My wife has serious charges hanging over her head. And I wasn't there for her. I should have been there," he said with such emotion that neither Oz nor Tope knew how to handle it. Alex being emotional was a rare event. "I was worried about my business collapsing when my own family was in more danger than any of my businesses could ever be." He shook his head. "I should have been here."

Then he steeled himself to go back inside that hospital room, but Oz stopped him. "Give her some space, Alexio. She'll come around. Just give her some space."

Alex didn't like being shut out like that. But now was not the time to stand on any principle. He did back off.

"Griff gave me a call with some news," said Tope.

Alex and Oz looked at him. "What is it?" asked Oz.

"We found a connection between Beverly Norgate and Dave Pantanzis."

"But how?" asked Oz. "We searched and found nothing."

"But Griff searched even deeper and found a connection in Pantanzis' cell phone records," said Tope. "Seems Pantanzis made several calls to an odd number we were able to trace back to Mrs. Norgate's cell phone the days leading up to the embezzlement and Galani Masarkis's disappearance."

"So there is a connection," said Oz. "You

weren't wrong, brother," he added, to Alex.

"At least Southeast is on their way now," said Oz.

Alex looked at him. "They rounded them all up?"

"Every one of them. They should be here soon."

But Alex was looking down the hall. When Oz and Tope looked too, they saw two men coming toward them. Oz placed his hand inside his pocket, in case he needed to defend somebody. The guards were on alert too.

But Alex could smell cop a mile away. They were a threat. But not like Oz and those bodyguards thought.

"Hello," said one of the men. He displayed his badge. "I'm Detective Herman. This is Detective Cousins. I need to speak with Mrs. Drakos."

"Do you guys have no shame?" asked Oz. "Her children were in a serious accident!"

"We understand that, sir. But we need to speak with her."

Oz looked at Alex. Alex nodded. Oz went and got Kari.

When Kari and Oz came out into the hall, Tope went inside with Jordan. Kari glanced at Alex. She was sorry that she overreacted. But she couldn't help it. Even her arrest wasn't enough to keep him around. "What is it?" she asked the detectives.

"We're here to inform you, ma'am, that your involvement with the shooting of Mr. Joseph Colburn has been determined to be a justifiable homicide and the state attorney will not pursue charges against you."

Alex was inwardly pleased. Kari was shocked. "But how? Once charges have been filed and bail set, doesn't a judge have to make that determination?"

"Normally yes," said the detective. "But the state attorney can refuse to prosecute. That's what happened."

"But why did they refuse? Did Sabrina recant her statement?"

"You mean your maid? No ma'am. We're unable to locate her, for one thing. But the main reason charges were dropped is because the governor got involved." They all looked at Alex at the mention of somebody that high up.

The detective nodded his head. "Have a nice day, ma'am," he said, and the two detectives left.

But everybody were still looking at Alex. Oz smiled. "You old fox! I knew you'd come up with something. That's where you were, wasn't it? In Tallahassee?"

Kari was staring at Alex. She was beating him up for not being there, when he was putting it all on the line to get those charges dropped? "Why didn't you just phone and tell me? Or tell Oz? Or tell *somebody*?"

"I wasn't certain it would pan out."

"That doesn't matter," Kari said, her face still trying to understand that wonderful, magnificent, ultra-aggravating husband of hers. "It's the action that counts, Alex. You tried to do something to help. It's always the action that counts!"

Alex just stood there flustered. Kari could feel his frustration. It was as if he was damned if he did, and damned if he didn't. Tears welled up in Kari's anguished eyes. "You should have told me," she said to him. But then she said, equally heartfelt, "Thank you."

Alex fought back his own brand of tears. "I just want our baby to be okay."

Kari saw the fear on his face. The fear she felt in her heart. The fear that their baby might not be okay, and it would kill them both. "Me too," she said as she went to him. He pulled her into his arms as she began sobbing.

"Me too," she said through her tears.

CHAPTER THIRTY-FOUR

An hour later and they were all sitting in Jordan's hospital suite. The only news they had received was the same old story: Angela was still in surgery.

Alex was seated in a chair against the wall, and Kari was on his lap. And remarkably, and to his delight because she was so stressed out, she had fallen asleep in his arms. Tope and Griff were also in the room.

Faye and Lucinda, Kari's closest friends, had dropped by, but had left when Kari had fallen asleep. All of the Gabrini families had phoned, to see if they were needed, but Alex had nodded no when Oz looked at him, so Oz thanked them for the offer but declined it. The Sinatras offered to help, too, including Big Daddy, but Oz declined their offers too. There wasn't anything more that anybody else could do. Oz had just gotten off of the phone with Big Daddy. "Jenay's back in the hospital."

"What's wrong with Jenay?" Kari asked.

"They think she might have Lupus or

219

some other issue, but Big Daddy seems to think those doctors are just guessing. Because she has some symptoms that lead them to say Lupus, but other symptoms that lead away from it being Lupus. She just gets so tired and sick sometimes. It's been going on for months now."

"I'm sorry to hear that," said Alex. "Charles never mentioned it to me."

"He wouldn't though, would he? Mick's the same way. Keeps shit all bottled up. He gets it from Big Daddy. And Gloria gets it from Mick."

Alex looked at Oz. He knew he and Gloria were having difficulties again. But it was so commonplace now that it was rarely mentioned. "Have their plane arrived yet?"

"Yep. They're on their way here now."

"Why didn't you meet their plane, Odysseus?"

"I'm not going anywhere until I know Angie's okay."

Alex stared at him. "Angela is my responsibility. Gloria and your daughter are your family. You need to worry about your responsibilities."

Oz and Alex exchanged a knowing look. They both were dropping the ball when it came to their responsibilities.

"I'm shocked Uncle Mick is coming," said

Jordan, who was sitting up in his hospital bed.

"I'm not surprised at all," said Alex. "He's a family man first and foremost."

Oz let out his one -syllable laugh. *Mick the Tick a family man*?" Even Tope and Griff were smiling. "Have you lost your mind, brother?" Then he turned to Griff, who knew Mick back in the day. "You ever hear something so crazy in your life, Griff?"

"That's a new one on me," said Griff as he grinned.

Oz looked at Tope. "What about you, Tope?"

"I don't personally know Mick Sinatra," said Tope, "but what I've heard of him don't lead me to think family man at all. I'm sorry, boss," he said to Alex with a grin, "but not at all."

"Even I know better than that, too, Daddy," said Jordan with a smile of his own. "I'm with Tope on that." Jordan and Tope were closer in age than of anybody else on his father's payroll, were both African-American, and as a consequence they naturally gravitated toward the other. They were allies.

But Alex stuck to his assessment. "No one has to agree with me," he said, "but I know what I'm talking about. I've seen that man in action. At the end of the day, Mick looks out for family."

Oz shook his head. "He don't be looking out for my family when he lets Glo continually run home to him every time we have a problem."

Nobody responded to that. Mainly because they all knew Oz liked the ladies, although they didn't think he had it in him to cheat on Gloria. But he certainly pushed the envelope much further than he should. Even Jordan had gotten on his beloved uncle's case about that very thing. There were two sides to Oz's story, and they weren't about to take one side without knowing about the other side.

"I spoke to Jovani," said Kari and everybody looked at her.

"How is she?" Jordan asked.

"She's fine. And so is Cate. Thankfully."

Alex nodded. "Yes."

The room door peered open. "Excuse me, sir," the guard said to Oz, "but your wife and father-in-law are coming up the hall now."

"Let them in," Oz said as he stood up, removed the hat on his head, and slung his long hair back. Then he put the hat back on. Tope and Griff stood up too. The very fact of seeing Mick the Tick in person gave Tope a charge. Griff had a different feeling about the man. He was a legend, that was a fact. He wasn't about to take away from Mick's legendary status. But he knew him as a bastard too. A man who would put a knife in your back if he even thought you crossed him.

As soon as Gloria Sinatra-Drakos and their daughter entered the room, and the little girl saw Oz, she ran to him. "Daddy!" she said happily. Alex looked at Kari on his lap. Despite the sudden commotion, she continued to sleep he was glad to see. She needed the rest.

"Hey," Oz said to Gloria as he held their daughter in his arms.

"Hey," Gloria said to Oz as she went over to him. "How's Angie?"

"Still in surgery."

"Damn. That's a long time in surgery."

"Tell me about it."

Then Mick Sinatra walked in. Jordan stared at him when he walked in. He did his research. He knew Uncle Mick was known as the boss of all mob bosses. The biggest of the big. And it showed on every inch of him. He terrified Jordan.

And everybody else, if they were to be honest. Because his mere presence, just walking in, changed the entire energy in the room. Whereas it had been warm before he arrived, now it felt as if he had brought in the cold.

But Alex, whom Mick viewed as his equal, smiled and extended his hand. "Hello,

Mick."

Mick went over to Alex and shook his hand. Alex Drakos was a man he respected above most men. "How are you?"

"Not good."

"She's still in?"

Alex nodded. "Yep. I had one of the best internal medicine surgeons around, a guy from John Hopkins, flown in. He's in there with the operating surgeons now. But he's reported back only that all appears to be going as it should, whatever the fuck that means."

"Doctors," Mick said, shaking his head.

But Alex was staring at him. "Thanks for coming. I didn't expect to see you. I figured you already had a thousand things on your plate."

"I have a million things on my plate," said Mick. "But family always comes first." Then he looked at Alex. "Right?"

Alex was suddenly uncomfortable with that look Mick was giving him, as if he knew all about his issues with Kari. As if Gloria had blabbed about that too. And he wondered if Oz was right when he insisted Gloria told her father *everything*. But regardless, Mick was right. Family did come first. "Right," Alex said, answering Mick's odd question.

Then Mick looked at Kari. "Takes balls to be able to sleep through this shit."

"Only just in the last half hour. She was a nervous wreck. I'm grateful she's getting some rest."

Mick nodded. Then he finally looked at Oz. And his look went from Mick's version of cordial, which to the naked eye would still seem cold, to downright cold. "Hello Odysseus."

Oz knew he was not one of Mick's favorite people lately. And no telling what Gloria had told him about their relationship. But whenever he called Oz by his full Christian name, it wasn't a good sign. "Good evening, Mick. How you doing?"

But Oz's baby girl started reaching for Alex. "I want to see Angie, Uncle Alex. I want to see Angie, Grandaddy," she said to Mick.

Oz and Gloria glanced at each other. It was as if their own daughter knew where the power center was in that room, and it wasn't either one of them. That bothered Oz. "You'll see her," he answered for his brother and father-in-law. "I guarantee it."

"Why would you promise her something you have no ability to guarantee?" Mick asked. "Don't write a check your ass can't cash."

Oz looked at Mick. "I never do," he said. "You, on the other hand--"

"That's enough," Alex interceded. "Both of you. This is not the time, Mick. And you know

225

it's not, Oz."

Both men backed down. Mick looked at Alex. "May I speak outside with you and Odysseus?"

"About?" Alex asked.

"The fuck-up that put your son and daughter in a hospital. The fuck-up that got somebody to set up your wife. Need I go on?"

Alex was shocked that Mick, too, saw connections. "No, you needn't," he said.

"You can discuss whatever you need to say in this room, Uncle Mick," said Jordan. "I'm no kid. And you'll get more privacy in here than anywhere else in this hospital."

Mick looked at Jordan. He was a smart young man who did everything the right way. Alex was going to make certain he went nowhere near that gangster life Mick and Oz and even Alex once upon a time were tied to. He was no gangster. But he was as tough as one. Mick liked him. But he looked at the non-relatives in the room. And his granddaughter.

"Gloria, you and Oz take your daughter for a walk. She's got bounds of energy still."

Gloria nodded. "Yes, sir," she said.

Oz didn't like taking instruction from Mick, especially when they weren't on good terms, but he understood the reasoning. And besides: he and Gloria still needed to talk. He sat his daughter on her own two feet, held her hand, and he and Gloria left the room.

Mick looked at the two non-relatives. "Griff I know," he said. "But who the fuck are you?" he asked Tope.

"That's Aaron Toparta," said Alex. "He's in charge of all of the security details for me and my family."

"So you're the one behind the latest fuck up," said Mick.

Tope thought he was going to throw up. He'd never been so scared in another man's presence in his life. "Yes, sir."

Mick didn't expect him to take ownership of it. But he was glad he did. "You knew Mrs. Drakos had been arrested when you dispatched a second detail to Jordan's school?"

"Yes, sir, I knew."

"You were aware that somebody had set her up?"

"Yes, sir, I was aware of it."

"Then why in hell did you let Jordan drive himself and his little sister?" Mick asked Tope.

"I . . . didn't think that there would be an issue with it, sir."

"Didn't think so, did you? Your thought wrong, didn't you?"

"I misjudged it, yes, sir."

"Misjudged it? Misjudged my ass! That's

a firing offense in my book," said Mick.

"Not in mine," said Alex.

Everybody looked at Alex. Especially Tope and Jordan.

"Tope is the best detail chief I've ever hired. And more importantly than that," Alex added, "he's a great human being. The fact that Jordan got in an accident and wasn't able to steer himself out of it isn't on Tope. That's on Jordan."

"Right," Jordan said, nodding his head. He would have been devastated had his father listened to Mick Sinatra and fired Tope.

"Or more specifically," Alex added with a frown on his face, "it's on me. Jordan is a brand-new driver. I should have been around to teach him more defensive maneuvers when blindsided, considering the family he's a member of. But I wasn't and I didn't. I'm not letting anybody, not even you, Mick, put that at Aaron's feet."

Tope inwardly sighed relief. Jordan did too. But they both looked at Mick. Alex had power, but Mick was Mick the Tick. As in ticking timebomb. As in liable to explode at any moment.

But Mick didn't explode. "If you have no problem with it, then so be it," he said to Alex, although it was obvious he didn't agree with it.

"But are you sold that it was an accident?"

Alex shook his head. "No. Not at all."

This surprised Jordan. Griff too. "Even though the background on the guy who hit J came back with no flags?" Griff asked.

"Fuck the background," Mick said. "They use regular people, with no blemishes on their records or their lives, to do their dirty work nowadays. Promise them riches or they have shit on them that could put them away for life."

"Who are *they*?" asked Griff.

"Whoever is behind this shit," Mick responded. "And I mean all of it."

"I've already reached that conclusion too," said Alex. "It's all connected somehow. I've been so worried about my baby that I haven't had a chance to figure out just what that connection could be."

"What about your southeast sector in Greece? A lot of money's missing. And so is your CEO."

Alex looked at Mick. How in hell did he know about that? "They're on their way. Under heavy escort."

"The entire board?"

"Yes."

Mick actually nodded his approval. "That's how you do that shit. Kidnap them. Get them out of their element. Get them on their knees begging for mercy. Good move, Drakos."

Jordan smiled. His old man impressed Mick the Tick? He was impressed with his old man!

Then the door opened again, and this time the surgeons who had actually performed the operation, and the surgeon Alex had flown in, walked into the suite. Oz, Gloria and the baby, who had seen the surgeons walk in, hurried in behind them.

Alex didn't hesitate waking Kari up for this.

"Did I fall asleep?" Kari asked as she was waking up.

"The surgeons are here babe," Alex said to her.

As soon as she saw the men in their scrubs, she quickly hopped off of Alex's lap and stood on her feet. Alex stood up too. Jordan sat up in his bed.

"How is she?" Kari asked them nervously.

"She's fine," the lead surgeon said, and everybody sighed relief.

"Thank you Jesus!" Jordan cried out.

But Kari wanted more details. "You say she's going to be fine, but what does that mean? What does that look like for her future?"

"There was internal bleeding, due to the

trauma of the car crash. But we were able to pinpoint the source and take care of it. But there's no lasting damage. There's no future surgeries that should ever be needed on this matter. She is expected to make a full and complete recovery."

Kari's legs buckled in relief and Alex and Mick grabbed hold of her. They sat her down in Alex's chair.

But Alex was looking at the surgeons. "We want to see her now," he said.

"She's still sedated and we recommend you wait--"

"Now." Alex made himself clear. "We won't disturb her. But her mother and I need to see her."

The surgeon nodded. "Yes, sir. If you'll follow me."

Alex looked at Kari. He already knew her answer. "I'm ready," Kari said, standing up though she was still wobbly. "I been ready."

And Alex helped her out of the room, down the corridor, and onto the elevator that took them and the lead surgeon, along with a bodyguard, downstairs to ICU.

When Alex and Kari saw their daughter, with tubes coming out of her tiny body in so many different directions, it still hurt them to their core. Kari leaned against Alex and Alex held onto Kari as it broke their hearts to see their baby that way. But she was going to be fine was the prognosis. And that was what they knew they had to focus on. That was what made them, for the first time in a long time, unabashedly happy and grateful.

CHAPTER THIRTY-FIVE

As Kari remained in ICU with Angela, and Oz and Tope remained in Jordan's room to oversee the family's security, Alex, Mick, and Griff went to the safe house where the Southeast board was being housed.

And as soon as they walked through that door, Alex didn't hesitate. He hurried over to Dave Pantanzis, and without saying a word, immediately began beating the crap out of him. Dave was screaming and trying to fight back, but his punches weren't landing. Alex didn't miss a punch.

The rest of the board were appalled, and rose to their feet in protest, as all they could hear was the deafening sounds of Alex's fist on Dave's flesh. They knew they had misappropriated funds, but it didn't take all this! Flying them across the world as if they were prisoners being extradited from their homeland to another country. Being treated like prisoners in this hellhole of a house. And now this?

One of them, a senior VP, had had enough. "Stop it at once!" he yelled. "This is barbaric!"

But before he could get out another word,

Mick pulled out his Magnum and shot him in the foot. "Shut the fuck up!" he yelled as the man began hopping and screaming in pain, and the rest of the board backed up. "Sit your asses down!" Mick ordered.

The rest of the board sat down without reservation. The senior VP, his cries muted in fear, sat down too as he took off his coat and wrapped his bleeding foot.

When Alex had administered the blow that seemed like the next to last blow that would have taken Dave away from here, he grabbed Dave up by his collar and spoke to him for the first time. "I want no bullshit," he said. "And once I ask, I'm not asking again. Who ordered you and this board to steal my money?"

Dave didn't bullshit, and he didn't hesitate either. The pain was too excruciating. "Mark did."

"Who the fuck is Mark?" asked Alex.

"McNeal," said Dave.

Griff was shocked. "Marcus McNeal?" he asked.

"Marcus?" asked Alex, stunned too. "My hotel's security chief?"

Dave nodded. "That's the one."

"Doesn't Aaron Toparta supervises him too?" asked Mick. "Isn't Tope his supervisor?"

"No," said Griff. "He's under my

jurisdiction."

"Then it's your ass that dropped the ball," said Mick.

But Alex needed answers. "Why would you listen to what some hotel security chief orders you to do?" he asked Dave.

"Because he had the goods on me," said Dave, his face bloodied and badly bruised. "He has the good on all of us. He had a book on me a mile long. It would have ruined me if I didn't do everything he told me to do. He had a book on every member of the board. We had no choice."

"Bullshit!" said Griff.

"What did he make you do?" asked Alex.

"He ordered me to get in touch with Bev Norgate, whom he knew your team was in negotiations with on that merger deal with her company. She was told to slow walk the deal. And to return to Budapest with one of her odd propositions so that you would be forced to fly to Hungary and deal with her there."

"What would my merger with Norgate have to do with you stealing from me?" asked Alex.

"To distract you."

"From what?"

"From focusing on the theft. To keep your mind on saving your conglomerate rather than on what happened to the eighty-percent of the southeastern sector's working capital that disappeared from the company's coffers. We're your smallest sector. That's why they picked on us."

"You orchestrated that theft?" asked Griff.

Dave nodded. "Yes. I needed buy-in from Walter Vokos and the rest of the board in order to pull it off, and they knew they had issues in their backgrounds too that would land them in even more trouble than embezzling funds."

"What did you do with the money?" Alex asked.

I was told to put the funds in an offshore account. The board thought they were going to get their share for their cooperation, but they weren't getting a dime. I wasn't either. It was all going to Mark McNeal. If he would have exposed me, I would have been doing a lifetime in prison. Compared to that, it was easy to say yes to this."

"What could he have had on any of you?" asked Griff. "My team did and continue to do extensive backgrounds on everybody who works for the Drakos Corporation."

"The shit he had on us would never show up on background. This only shows up when somebody plants cameras in your house. He planted plenty in all of our houses."

Alex didn't even want to know the twisted shit Dave and that board was involved in. He just wanted answers that would make his family safe again. He wanted to know who the head honcho was. He knew for damn sure it wasn't Marcus McNeal.

He looked at Griff. "Call the hotel. Find out where Marcus is and get a detail to detain him until we can get there."

"He's not at the hotel anymore," Griff said.

Alex looked at him. "What do you mean?"

"I fired him when Mrs. Drakos was arrested. He didn't take photos of the crime scene and he didn't get that maid on tape telling exactly what happened should the cops show up and hide evidence or get witnesses to lie just so they could arrest a Drakos. He knew the protocol when it involves a family member. And he did none of that. I had no choice but to relieve him of his duties."

Alex couldn't argue with Griff's decision. But it only made their job harder. He looked at Dave. "Where's McNeal now?"

Dave shook his head. "I don't know. We haven't heard from him since the money was placed in that offshore account. That was all I had to do."

"And Walter Vokos?"

Dave looked at Frank Savalas, the security chief for Southeast. He was as terrified as Dave. "Walter was getting scared. Dave and me knew he was the weak link, so I called Mark. He told me to hire an assassin to take him out. So I did."

"So Walter was in on it too?"

Dave nodded. "We all were."

"Including Galani?" asked Alex.

Dave shook his head. "No. We don't know what happened to her. I asked McNeal once, but he told me that wasn't my business. He told me no matter what we said, we had to always put the blame for that missing money on Galani. And that's what we did."

Alex exhaled. He looked at Griff. "I want Marcus found and brought to this house. He'll more than likely be in hiding somewhere now, so it won't be easy. But find him."

"We will," Griff assured him.

Then Alex and Mick began to leave. Mick was looking at Alex, as if he forgot his clothes. Griff went up to him too.

"What do we do with this bunch?" Griff asked. "Do we take'em out?"

Alex looked at Griff. "You work them over. They deserve that. But you don't kill them."

"And then?" asked Griff.

"And then I'll fire them."

Griff and Mick both seemed disappointed.

But Alex was firm. "I'm not running a mob syndicate where somebody dies just from disrespecting me. I'm running a corporation. And in my world, the punishment will fit the crime. They stole money. They will remain here until I'm confident their story checks out and I have access to that offshore account. And then they will be fired. That's how this works. Understood?"

"Yes, sir," said Griff.

Mick smiled. "Griff's old school like my ass. I wish those fuckers would take my money and live to tell about it."

Alex knew in Mick's world his decision not to kill his board would be considered a bitch-ass move. But he was out of that world and was never going back. He despised that world. "I'm not you, and I'm not Griff." Then the looked at Griff again. "Find Marcus," he said, and left.

CHAPTER THIRTY-SIX

Three days later, Angela was released from the hospital, joining her parents and her brother, who'd been released two days earlier, back home. Alex and Kari had remained at the hospital together during Angie's entire hospital stay and both were relieved, but emotionally spent.

Faye and Lucinda came over, along with Oz and his family, and they all spent the better part of the day at the penthouse. Mick left town after it was obvious it would take some time to find Marcus McNeal, and Oz and Gloria laughed and talked with everybody but each other. It was as if nothing, with them, had been resolved.

But that was their problem. Alex and Kari were too drained to even care.

That night, after everybody had gone home and Angie and Jordan had gone to bed, they took a long tub bath together and then spent their evening up on rooftop terrace where they reclined together in one lounge, sipped champagne, and relaxed. Kari wore Alex's big shirt with panties because she was outside. Alex wore a pair of pants and no shirt. They were comfortable.

After several minutes of silence, Alex spoke what had been on his mind for some time. "He never called, did he?"

Kari looked at Alex. But then she sipped her champagne. She could have played dumb and pretend she didn't know who he was talking about, but that wasn't her style. She said nothing.

"That figures," said Alex. "Some friend."

"He was no friend," said Kari. "Diallo Koffi was going to be my business partner. I was in it because I was afraid that I needed to get in it."

Alex looked at her. "Afraid of what?"

"Of losing you. Of ending up with two children to raise and depending on a man for support who doesn't want to have anything to do with me."

"Oh, Kari, I would never--"

"I know you're saying that. Every man says that shit until after the divorce, and then all that support gets real old real fast. I wasn't going to allow myself to depend on that. I saw going into business with Dee as a way to provide for myself and my kids. That's all I was in it for."

"And?" Alex said, and then looked at her. "Were you in it to see if there could be a future with Diallo too?"

Kari hesitated. "If your ass wouldn't have acted right, who knows?"

Alex loved her honesty, even though it hurt. And he frowned. Kari could feel his anxiety. She looked at him.

It'll never happen again, Karena," he said. "I'll never put anything ahead of you and our children ever again."

"Words are cheap, Alex. I've heard those words before."

"My actions will speak for me. How about that?"

Kari lifted her glass. "I'll take it."

"And from here on out," he said to her, "we do everything together. If I have to go on a business trip, you and the children are going with me. If they have to miss school, we'll have tutors traveling with us. Whatever it takes. We'll stand or fall as a family. We're going to do everything as a family. I almost lost you guys," Alex said as great emotion could be heard in his voice. "That won't ever happen again."

Kari stared at Alex. And like all those other times, she believed him. Because she knew him. She knew he loved them. She knew he would do nothing to hurt them. Now he had to prove that he would go to the ends of the earth to help keep them together. His actions will speak for him. They were starting with a clean slate.

That was why Kari knew she had to tell Alex the truth. "Actually, Dee did call," she said to him.

Alex looked at her. "Diallo Koffi called you?"

"Several times after the kids had their accident," said Kari. "But I never answered any of his calls."

"Why not?"

"I didn't want to confuse the picture. Or him or anybody else. Our children were in trouble. This was between me, you, and our children. Third parties had to back the fuck up."

Alex smiled. He lifted his glass this time. "Agreed," he said. "From here on out, we're in this together," said Alex. "No matter what."

But in the meantime, Kari knew how stressed the last few days had been for Alex and for herself too. She sat her glass of champagne on the side table, lifted her butt and removed the panties beneath Alex's big dress shirt she wore, tossed them aside, and she got on top of him, straddling him and facing him.

Alex, pleased, sat his glass of champagne on the side table too, and pulled down his pants. And they began kissing as Alex unbuttoned her shirt and began fondling her breasts as they kissed.

Until he moved down and began to kiss her breasts, too, as his fingers moved between her legs and massaged her.

And as soon as he could feel her wetness, he didn't hesitate. He put it inside of her with a slow, passionate entrance that got her going early. It felt as if she was on the verge of cumming as soon as she felt his entry.

But Alex knew how to keep it slow and easy. And he did. He pressed the button that leaned the back of the lounger nearly prone, and he laid Kari down on top of him. And he wrapped her in his arms and made love to her, with slow and steady gyrations, for over half an hour. And he, too, felt as if he was going to orgasm at any moment the entire time. It was wonderful to both of them.

And then they came. Together. But what had been slow and easy turned into a dynamic cum. They both let out moans and groans and Alex captured Kari's mouth again, as they came.

But just as they were easing from the height of their cum, Alex's phone rang.

Alex was too far gone, still pouring inside of her even as it was easing off, but Kari looked at the Caller ID. When she saw that it was Griff, she answered. "Just a minute, Griff," she said.

She waited until Alex had poured out all he could pour out inside of her. It felt just that good. And then she handed him the phone.

"Shit," he said anyway, as he answered. "Yeah?"

"We found Marcus," said Griff over the phone.

That was what Alex wanted to hear.

"We got that motherfucker. He's here at the house awaiting your arrival."

"I'm on my way," Alex said. Then he thought about it, and looked at Kari. "*We're* on our way," he said, and ended the call.

Kari was staring at him. "We? As in me?"

"Everything together," said Alex. "Remember?"

"But what about the children?"

"Oz and Gloria live at The Drakos. They'll come up here in no time flat to stay with the children until we get back. Together, Kari. That's not just vain words. I'm going to that safe house to deal with something that affects *our* family, not just *my* family. *Our* family. Everything together. Let's stay together."

Kari smiled. "I'll love to," she said, they kissed, and he eased out of her as she got up off of him.

CHAPTER THIRTY-SEVEN

A limousine, followed by an SUV, drove around a boarded-up factory on the southside of Apple Valley and parked beside a white cargo van. Two men got out of the front seat of the van, went around back, and opened the double doors.

Marcus McNeal, the head of hotel security at The Drakos, recoiled when the door was opened. He was already badly beaten, and behaved as if he was expecting more of the same. The two men then grabbed him and began pulling him out of the van as a bodyguard got out from the front passenger seat of the limo and opened the back passenger door. The two men flung Marcus into that limo, causing him to land on the seat right beside his former boss, Griffin Coles. But Griff was the least of his worries. Alex and Kari Drakos were seated across from Marcus and his boss.

"They almost killed me," Marcus complained. "Like I'm some traitor. When I haven't done anything."

"An innocent man doesn't run," said Griff. "You ran when they approached you. Better be glad they didn't kill your ass."

"But what did I do?!"

"Why did you order Dave Pantanzis to embezzle eighty-percent of my working capital in my southeastern sector?" Alex asked, and then he and Kari stared at him. They knew him well. They trusted him before they found out his part in this sordid mess. It was difficult.

And although they were certain Marcus had to have known the gig was up or he wouldn't be in front of them that way, they were pissed that he didn't own his shit. He kept the charade going. "I didn't order Dave Pantanzis or anybody else to do anything. Who told that lie on me?"

Kari shook her head and looked at Alex. How were they going to get a morsel of truth out of this guy? But Alex removed his arm from around her waist and moved up to the edge of his seat. He stared directly into Marcus's swollen eyes. "You ordered Dave to steal my money and transfer every dime to that offshore account that you and you alone have access to. On that there is no doubt. You also ordered the hit on my southeast CFO, Walter Vokos. On that there is also no doubt. So cut the bullshit. The only thing I need you to tell me, and the only thing I'm interested in hearing from you, is why did you do it, and who ordered you to do it."

If Marcus came in with attitude, it was

quickly fading away. His entire demeanor began to change. "It was to finance the operation," he said.

Kari scooted to the edge of her seat too. "What operation?"

Marcus looked at Kari and tears welled up in his eyes. "I'm sorry, Mrs. Drakos. You were a very good employer. You were very good to me."

Alex anger flared. "What operation? Answer her question."

"Operation Family Drop," said Marcus.

Griff frowned. "What the fuck kind of operation is that?"

"What does it mean?" asked Alex.

Marcus knew this was where the confession got scary. He didn't respond right away.

"What does it mean, Marcus?" asked Kari. He wasn't about to escape that question, and he had to know it.

"Tell us what Operation Family Drop means," said Alex.

Marcus exhaled, and then just went on and said it. "It means we were tasked with ensuring that your wife, your son Jordan, your daughters Cate and Angela, and your granddaughter Jovani were eliminated," he said.

Alex's heart dropped. So did Kari's.

"*Eliminated*?" Kari asked, the shock visible on her face and heard in her voice. "All of us?"

"Yes."

"Why?" she asked.

"So that your husband would be free."

Kari frowned. So did Griff. And they both looked at Alex.

But Alex was still staring at Marcus. "Free to do what?" he asked him.

Marcus shook his head. "That was where my knowledge begins and ends. I blackmailed your southeast sector to embezzle that money and put it in an account offshore. I paid that maid and Joe Colburn to pretend to be victim and rapist when you were on the same floor as the room Joe was occupying. It was a fake knife, but when you entered that suite and hurried to rescue your maid, he was hired to take you out. He would drop the fake knife, pull out his gun, and take you out. But you took him out before he could do anything."

"So Colburn was a hit man?" Alex asked.

"He was a greedy man willing to perform a hit for money, yes, sir. He had no record. Nothing to pull up red flags. He was perfect for the operation."

"So you're telling me you hired him to kill my wife?"

Marcus knew it wasn't going to sit right

with Drakos. "Yes, I was ordered to hire a hit man."

"Where's the maid now?" asked Kari. She knew, like Alex knew, to keep him talking before they forced him to give up the ringleader. "The cops can't find her."

"They won't find her either. She's at the bottom of the ocean. She did her part, but she knew too much."

"What about that shooting at the mall? You were behind that too?" Alex asked.

Marcus shook his head. "Not at all. I knew nothing about that. You can't put that mall shit on me. And you were wrong about one other thing, too, Mr. Drakos."

Alex didn't respond. He waited for Marcus to tell him where he was wrong.

"I wasn't the only person with access to that offshore account."

This intrigued all of them because they knew Marcus was about to give up the name of the ringleader. "Who else had access?" Alex asked him.

"The woman that hired me. The same woman that ran your southeastern sector."

Griff frowned. "Galani Masakis?"

Marcus nodded. "Galani. That's her. She's the one that approached me, promising me millions if I succeeded in getting those funds into that offshore account, and getting rid of Mrs. Drakos. And getting her lost until Mr. Drakos was distracted elsewhere."

"Distracted," said Griff. "That word again."

"Distracted how?" asked Kari.

"Distracted as in grieving the loss of his entire family. Then she'd resurface, claiming to have been kidnapped and badly beaten or some shit like that. And then she'd claim her rightful place beside you, sir," Marcus said, looking at Alex.

Alex just sat there. To say that he and Galani Masakis were close would be an understatement. They grew up together. He regarded her as a sister. But it still wasn't adding up.

"I know you don't believe she could be involved," Dave said. "But she is. She's behind all of it. You and her are tight. Everybody in Southeast knows that."

Kari didn't know it. She'd never heard of the woman before. The southeast sector in Greece was one of their smallest subsidiaries.

"She's wanted you for decades," Marcus continued. "And with your entire conglomerate in even more trouble than it had been in almost all those previous times, she saw an opening." He grimaced, as the pain of those licks Alex's guys had laid on him were beginning to sting again. "And decided to exploit it."

"Where is she now?" Alex asked.

Marcus shook his head. "I don't know."

"Bullshit."

"I don't know! All she said was that she'd be hiding in plain sight. Right under your nose. That's all she said. I don't know where she is."

After it was clear Marcus would have nothing more of value to offer, he nodded to Griff. Griff began getting out of the car. "Let's go," he said to Marcus.

As Marcus was pulled out by the two men from the van, Alex looked at Kari. "I'll be back," he said, and got out of the limo and got into the van. Griff closed the van doors, with Alex inside with Marcus.

Marcus was thrown on the van's floor as Alex got onto the van behind him. When the door closed, he began scooting backwards on his butt.

Alex began putting on a pair of gloves.

"You can't harm me," said Marcus. "You're not like that. Galani said you weren't like that. She said you left your gangster lifestyle behind."

"She's right. I did."

"Then why are you pulling out that gun?" Terror was in Marcus's eyes.

"There's no way an individual is going to tell me that he hired a hitman to murder my wife, and not expect to be murdered himself." Alex raised the gun, aimed it, and fired five times.

Marcus was gone, and his scream was an echo, by shot number two.

Kari heard the gunshots, and she knew what was happening. She also knew Alex wouldn't do it if he had a choice.

And that was why, when Alex and Griff returned to the limo, and Alex leaned his head back as if that level of violence he had hoped remained in his past, Kari placed her hand around his thick arm and leaned against him. He took his arm, put it around her waist, and took solace in knowing she was there for him. That they were on the same page.

But as they slowly began to drive away, Alex thought about what Marcus had said. And then he realized what that could only mean. "I'll be damn."

"What?" Kari asked.

"Take me home," Alex said to his driver. "Take me home now!"

The driver, hearing the urgency in the boss's voice, sped up.

"What is it, Alex?" Griff asked. Kari wanted to know too.

But Alex was phoning his hotel's front

desk. "This is Alex Drakos. Tell me if we have a Gail Browne registered."

"One moment, sir, while I check."

While Alex waited, he looked at Kari. "It was always the name she used when we would meet up at hotels."

Griff knew what that meant. Kari knew what it meant too. Alex was too engrossed to realize Kari had only suspected that he and Galani had been lovers before. Now it was confirmed.

But it still confused her. "But you're calling *our* hotel," she said. "You can't believe she'd be bold enough to be hiding out in *our* hotel."

"In plain sight? Under my nose? She couldn't get any closer, or plainer than right at The Drakos."

Kari realized it too. So did Griff. "I'll be doggone," Griff said.

"Mr. Drakos?"

"Yes, I'm still here," Alex said to the woman on the other end of his phone.

"We do indeed have a Gail Browne registered here. She's in room 653."

They all were shocked. Room 653 was the very suite next door to the scene where Kari was forced to shoot to defend her maid.

"Okay thank you," Alex said and ended

the call. He and Kari looked at each other. They could hardly believe it.

CHAPTER THIRTY-EIGHT

They found out that not only was she registered under the name of Gail Browne, but they also discovered that she had her breakfast, lunch, and dinner delivered by room service every day at the exact same time.

Deciding to wait until morning, they went to the penthouse. But a security detail observed the outside of her suite on security cameras through the night. Nobody came or went. And when it was time for her breakfast to be delivered to her, Alex and Kari, along with Griff, took the tray, went upstairs, and knocked on her door.

Galani Masakis, accustomed to the routine, opened the door without hesitation. "I am starved," she said as she usually said at breakfast delivery. But as soon as she saw that it was Alex Drakos and his wife at her door, a look of horror appeared on her face and she quickly attempted to close the door back. But Alex already had his big shoe in the way. He, Kari, and Griff walked on in, instead, and closed and locked the door.

Galani was backing up. "What do you want?"

But Griff walked in and began frisking Galani for weapons. "Are you serious?" Galani asked, but allowed the frisk.

Then Griff began looking around the one-bedroom suite to make sure nobody else was inside. Kari just stood beside Alex, staring at Galani. She was definitely a beautiful woman. Very desirable. She could understand why somebody like her would feel she was entitled to have the best like Alex. Because Alex was desirable too. But to concoct such an elaborate plan just to get a man? It made no sense to Kari.

"What do you want, Alexio?" Galani asked Alex again.

But Alex waited until Griff gave the all-clear before he spoke. When Griff returned up front with a thumbs up, Alex looked at his sector CEO. "We aren't playing games with you. I'm here. In your hiding place. That means the gig is up. The only question to be answered is why would you plot to have my entire family murdered? Because you were behind those car crashes too. Weren't you?"

Galani smiled a weak, troubled smile. "No matter what I did," she said. Kari could see the look of regret in her bright blue eyes. She was tired of the game too. "My husband committed suicide."

Alex frowned. "That was nearly twenty

years ago. And I stood by your side that entire time."

"I know you did. I knew you would. But he knew the truth."

"Who knew the truth?" When she wouldn't answer that question yet, Alex posed another one. "What truth?"

"That it wasn't. . . That my husband didn't kill himself." Then she looked at Alex. "He found out that I did."

Alex's already large eyes opened larger. Even Kari was shocked. "Are you telling me that you killed Jack?" Alex was staring at her. "Are you telling me that Jack didn't commit suicide?"

Galani closed her eyes as if she could close the truth away, then she opened them again. "That's what I'm telling you, yes. And he found out about it."

"Wait. Who?" asked Kari. "Who found out about it?"

Galani gave Kari a hard stare. "You," she said. "You're where I've always wanted to be. And even after I killed my husband, who was a very good man, it didn't get me Alex. He had no problem fucking me. But he wasn't interested in anything more from me. So I stayed around and accepted the crumbs. Year in and year out. Until even I got tired of crumbs. I wanted more. When the conglomerate was on life support again, I decided to go for broke. I decided to put it all on the line."

She looked at Kari again. "You didn't have to do anything to win Alex's heart. You beat us all, and you didn't even have to try."

Kari could tell Alex was affected by her pain. But Kari didn't know the bitch from a hole in the wall. And they needed answers. If this shit didn't stop with her, then who did it stop with? "Who found out that you killed your husband?" Kari asked her.

Galani's look changed. "He'll be here any moment. He always has breakfast with me. And we strategize. It's called hiding in plain sight."

"Who are you talking about, motherfucker?" asked Griff, who patience with Galani was waning. "Just tell us who."

"The one who took on his wife's name," said Galani. "Such a punk-ass move, but it got him the attention he craved."

Alex knew that couldn't be right. "What are you saying?"

Galani smiled. "It's gets better and better, doesn't it? But I didn't stutter. I'm talking about Matthew Stafford-Scribner. Or is it Scribner-Stafford? Whatever. Your former CFO. Your former close friend."

Before Alex could respond to the

shocking news, knocks were heard on the suite door. Galani smiled. "I told you he would be here like clockwork. I'm a lot of things. But I'm no liar."

"A murderer who covers up her crimes is a liar," said Kari. "And a murderer."

Galani's smile left.

Griff went to the door and looked out of the peephole. He looked at Alex shocked. "I'll be damned."

Alex hurried over to the peephole himself. And when he looked through it and saw that it was indeed Matthew Stafford-Scribner, his former friend and the CFO he was compelled to fire, he was stunned too. And angry as hell. He flung open that door.

When Matthew saw his former friend and boss, it was obvious he had been blindsided. And he didn't hesitate. Unlike Galani and Dave, who pretended all was still well, he knew it wasn't. He was in a baseball cap and now sported a beard, his identity concealed enough to get into The Drakos undetected, but he went the back ways up anyway. Because he knew, even with a beard and cap, Alex would know him anywhere. That was why, as soon as he saw Alex's face in Galani's suite, he did the only thing he knew he had left: he pulled his weapon, fired a shot into the room that forced Alex to back away, and he took off running.

Alex looked at Griff. "What you wanted to do to Southeast? It's appropriate to do now," he said, and then he took off running after Matthew.

Griff got on the phone to security downstairs, to alert them to try and assist in the capture, and then he looked at Galani.

"What are you going to do to me?" she asked nervously when Griff pulled out his weapon.

"What you tried to do to Alex's family," Griff responded without hesitation. He began putting a silencer on his gun.

Kari had run out of the hotel room too. But as Alex went one way toward the back stairs where Matthew was running, Kari went the opposite way, toward the elevators. She knew, like Alex knew, that Matthew knew the back ways. He knew his way around The Drakos. That was probably how he was able to visit Galani daily, and remain undetected.

Alex ran down the stairs behind Matthew. He was faster than his old friend, and knew he could make up a lot of territory. But as soon as Matthew, who was still running fast, began to hear Alex's footsteps approaching even faster, he stopped and turned and fired his weapon, thinking Alex would retreat. But Alex, instead, fired at Matthew. He didn't want to hit him. He needed answers from him. Because all of this carnage couldn't possibly be for the reason Dave and Galani gave. Was it just pure revenge on Matthew's part?

But as the stairwell door opened on the lower level, and Alex's hotel security team began to run up toward him, Matthew immediately took a keycard that was supposed to have been returned to the corporation when he was let go, a key even the rank and file security didn't have, and he swiped it across the side wall and a door opened. Matthew then ran through that door and down the final steps that led outside.

The door closed by the time Alex, coming downstairs, and his hotel security staff, coming upstairs, made it to the side wall. But Alex used his key, the door opened again, and they all ran behind Matthew.

But by the time they got outside into the side parking lot, Matthew was hopping into his Jaguar and speeding away.

But Kari had driven around, from the private garage, in her Mercedes, and she rammed the Jag just as it was about to get onto the highway. It worked. She jammed it and Alex and Security were able to run up to it.

But Matthew was a well-experienced

driver. He was able to correct, back away from the Mercedes, and speed away just as Alex was reaching for the door.

Alex hopped into the Mercedes, and Kari sped after Matthew. The security detail car onsite sped out of the parking lot, too, and chased behind Alex and Kari.

Matthew drove like a man determined to get away or die trying. Which made him so dangerous that Alex told Kari not to risk too much. And he got on his phone and ordered the security detail car behind them to get in front. They were paid high dollar to do this shit. He wasn't letting his wife risk her life doing their job.

The detail car got in front of the Mercedes the first chance they could and were able to drive even faster than Kari was driving. But they still wasn't making much headway as Matthew was tearing in and out of lanes, nearly hitting car after car, as it drove to break free.

Alex and Kari were able to keep an eye on the car, as he turned down side road after side road, until Kari broke away from the tail and took a different road.

"What are you thinking?" asked Alex.

"He's headed for Airport Road."

"You think he's going to try to fly out of town?"

"Maybe. But that's where he appears to

be heading. And I know a shortcut," Kari said as she sped down a narrow stretch of highway.

But while they were speeding up to the road that intersected where Kari believed Matthew was heading, they heard what sounded like a horrific crash.

"Go!" yelled Alex and Kari put on the afterburners as she sped up to the intersection.

And that was when they saw the wreck. Matthew had literally wrapped his car around a pole. The security team jumped out and ran to the car as Kari drove up.

Alex and Kari jumped out, too, and ran to the car.

"He's still alive, Boss!" one of the guards said. "But barely."

Alex ran up to Mathew.

He was barely there. The guard was right. "Why, Matt?" asked Alex with strain in his voice. "Why would you want to destroy my family? Because I fired you?"

But Matthew was looking at him, shaking his head. And Alex realized Matthew was not the vengeful type. He was a sensitive man who took on his wife's name to appease his wife for crying out loud.

And a different thought occurred to Alex. Maybe it didn't end with Galani and Matthew. "Who's behind this, Matt? Tell me who's behind this?"

Kari looked at Alex. What was he talking about? How could he think it would be somebody else?

But he was apparently on the right track because Matthew grabbed his shirt. And with the little breath he had left, he said the name. "Cate," he said. "Cate is the one. She's hates," he started saying, but then his breath was gone.

But he could have saved his breath. Alex knew what he was going to say. Cate hated him. As in Alex. As in her father.

But he was still frozen in place. Kari was too. Did he just say Cate? Alex's Cate? Did he just say Alex's daughter was the mastermind?

"But how can that be?" asked a confused Kari. "She and the baby were nearly killed too."

But Alex was thinking in every direction. And he knew his daughter was capable of evil. He thought she was over it. He thought she had changed. But evil was easy to disguise.

And an evil, hellbent person would risk everything, including her own baby, to gain what her twisted mind believed would be everything else: Alex's heart because she and Jovani would be all he had left of his immediate family. And, more importantly, she could worm her way back into his money.

He looked at Kari as police cars arrived.

And that look alone made it clear to her that it was no mistake. Alex was certain Cate was involved.

CHAPTER THIRTY-NINE

"I like that one."

"The blue one?"

"Yep."

"Why the blue baby giraffe and not the purple one?"

"Because the blue one looks like he needs a friend."

"Ah," said Kari. "That is so sweet!" And she reached over and kissed her baby girl.

Alex smiled too. They were sitting up in Angela's bed with Angela in the middle between them. And she was pointing out every toy she wanted from the Amazon website pulled up on her iPad. It was a long list.

"Hey guys." Jordan came into the bedroom plopped down across the foot of the bed.

"Where have you been?"

"Downstairs in the casino with Uncle Oz. But he had to make a run."

Alex nodded. Oz was making a run for him. "Didn't I tell you to stay out of that casino?"

"I wasn't gambling, Dad. I was just hanging out with my uncle. So until Uncle Oz gets back, I thought I'd take Ang up to the roof to shoot some hoops with me."

"She just got out of the hospital, J," said Kari. "Not yet."

"Oh please, can I go?" Angela loved shooting hoops with Jordan.

"Not right now," said Alex. "Find something else to do with your brother."

Angela looked at Jordan with a smile on her face.

"Not that video game again," said Jordan.

"Please," said Angela.

Jordan shook his head. He needed to lose weight, and he wasn't going to lose it sitting in front of a television screen.

But for Angela? "Okay, let's do it," he said and Angela quickly got out of bed and went with her brother to the game room.

"And Jordan?"

Jordan turned around.

"Stay off the roof for a while."

"But why? I already feel like a prisoner in my own home. The only reason I got to go downstairs was because I went with Oz. But as soon as he had to leave, he had Tope escort me back upstairs like I'm some kid."

"Or the kid of somebody with enemies," said Alex. "Which is what you are. You and Angela will do exactly as we say. You hear me?"

Jordan nodded. "Yes, sir." Then he stared at his father.

Alex was staring back. "What?"

"You're going to stick around this time?"

A part of Alex didn't like the question and wanted to tell Jordan so. But the bigger part of him knew exactly why Jordan asked it. "Yes," he said. "I'm sticking around."

Jordan looked at his mother.

"He's sticking around," she said. "He's going to stick around so much you're going to get tired of him."

Jordan smiled. "I doubt that," he said, and he and Angela began heading out of the room.

But Angela turned back and looked at her parents. "Don't be sad," she said. "I'll be back."

"Okay," said Kari.

"We're try our best," said Alex.

But when Angela and Jordan left the room, Alex and Kari broke out into laughter. "She's full of herself, isn't she?" Alex said.

"Just like her father," said Kari, and Alex wrapped his arm around her neck and pretended to put her in a chokehold.

But then their gaiety turned into their somberness as they thought about the matter at hand. Kari looked at Alex. "What if we're wrong?" she asked. "What if Matthew didn't know what he was saying."

"He wouldn't have said it if he didn't know," said Alex.

"But why would he be caught up in a scheme to kill your family? You and he used to be so close."

Alex exhaled. "I don't know. But I'm going to find out."

"And you're certain Cate is behind all of this?"

It was a painful reality. "Yes," said Alex.

"But what would be her reason?"

"The same thing it's always been with Cate: money. Namely my money and how she can control more of it."

"As generous as you've been to her and she wants more?"

"My generosity doesn't scratch the surface with that girl," said Alex. "She's never been satisfied a day of her entire life."

Then the intercom buzzed. Alex pressed the button on the nightstand. "Yes?"

"It's me, Brother." It was Oz. "I'm downstairs getting ready to head up. I have Jovani with me."

Alex closed his eyes. Then he opened them and nodded. "Okay," he said, and released the button.

Then he laid there another few seconds, staring into nothingness. Because he knew it was time. Cate's final day of reckoning. And then he got out of bed.

Kari could feel his heaviness. She got out of bed too. "Alex, let me go with you."

"No. No way. "I created this monster. I'm the only one that can put it down."

"You're the one who said we were together. That we would do everything, and you meant *everything*, together. Not just in good times. But in all times. This is that time. This is especially that time."

Alex looked at Kari. Before she said those words, there was no way he was taking her with him. But she was right. He couldn't coddle her. His word had to be what it was supposed to be and not situational. He had to put up or shut up.

He nodded his head, and left the room. Kari, relieved, hurried behind him.

CHAPTER FORTY

When Cate Drakos saw her father and stepmother at her front door, she answered quickly. "Did something happen?" she asked. "Oz came and picked up Jo. Did something happen?"

"No," said Kari. "Jovani's fine."

"Oh. Thank God! Come on in." She opened the door further and allowed Alex and Kari to walk on in. Her relaxed demeanor would have fooled most people. But Alex and Kari had seen it too many times. It didn't fool them.

"Have a seat. Would you guys like something to drink?"

"No," said Alex as they sat down on her sofa.

Cate hesitated, because of his curt tone, but she closed the door anyway and went and sat in the chair by the sofa. "So what's going on? I wanted to come to the hospital to see Angie, but Tope wouldn't let me. And Uncle Oz backed him up. But why are you guys here now? Jo isn't here. And Daddy never comes just to see me. If he bothers to come at all, it's always to pick up Jovani."

Alex and Kari just stared at her, as if they

were trying with all their might to figure her out. She didn't like it. "Are you guys going to tell me what's going on or what?"

"Why don't you tell us," said Kari.

"I don't know what you're talking about to tell you anything."

"Let's start with my southeast sector," said Alex. "Or maybe Bev Norgate. Or maybe Marcus McNeal. Or maybe Galani. Or maybe Matthew."

Kari could tell Cate was shocked that they knew as much as they did. Her facial expression changed. "I don't understand."

"Yes your ass do," said Alex. "You understand exactly what I'm talking about. You initiated Operation Family Drop. Didn't you?"

Cate just sat there.

"No point in lying anymore, Cate," said Kari. "We know the story or we wouldn't be here."

It was only then did Cate's true personality began to break through. "So what if it is true?" She folded her arms. "So what? We tried. We failed."

"You had access to an offshore account that I've already shut down."

She unfolded her arms. "You can't shut anything down! It's not in your name."

"But I did. And all of your minions who

did your bidding because you managed to spy on them and get the goods on them have told everything they know. Everything," said Alex with bitterness in his voice.

Cate sat up defiantly. "I'm not going back to prison!"

"Why did you do it?" asked Kari. She was genuinely confused by this girl. "Your father has been so kind to you."

"Kind? Are you on dope? He's a billionaire and he throws me and his only grandchild crumbs. Crumbs I tell you! While you and your brats get all the jewels. I don't want anybody's crumbs. I'm his daughter. I deserve better than that! And you wanna know why I did it? Because I saw you, one day, driving around town in your Bentley and with Fast Faye and Lush Lucinda in the car right along with you. Spending Daddy's money like it's your birthright. And was just getting a little a month like me and Jo were his pets. I said no way. I got to get your ass out of the way, and that big-headed baby of yours, and that flat-face boy of yours all out of the way. Then it'll be just me, Daddy, and Jo. So when Daddy was gone all the time because of the recession, I got busy. Hired some private eyes to get the dirt on who I needed to accomplish my goals, and not one of them turned me down. But they never knew it was me. Dave thought it was just Marcus. Marcus thought it was just Galani. Galani thought was just Matthew. That was how brilliant I worked it. Matthew was the only one who knew it was me. Because I had to make him do it. I had to give him an offer he couldn't refuse."

"Which was?"

"His wife's life in exchange for his cooperation. He didn't cooperate, she was going to be killed. And he knew I'd do it too. He knew you would never stop me or you would have long ago. He knows you're no killer. I know it too. You'd never harm your own child."

She smiled. "I even hired that mass shooter in the mall to try and take Kari out. But his stupid ass let some African take him out. And all those people died and you lived. How whacked is that?"

Alex was listening to his daughter as if he was listening to pure evil. She had no conscience. She had no soul. She had no concept of love and devotion and family. But yet he spared her, time and time and time again. How could he have let this go on this long? How could he have continued to put his family at risk believing that she could change, that she would somehow be that innocent little girl he remembered? This shitstorm was on him. And him alone.

"Karena," he said, "wait outside."

Kari wanted to argue with Alex. She wanted to insist that she should be there with him. Together. But that look in his eyes told her he did not want to have to sink as low as he had to sink, and have her witness what was truly going to be a part of him dying too.

She stood up to leave. Alex stood up too. But Cate, whose singular talent was not being able to read a room, wasn't getting it at all. She stood up as well. "Why does she have to leave?" she asked. "You can say what you wanna say to my face."

"You fool," said Kari. "He doesn't have anything to say to you. Don't you realize that?"

Alex began putting on his gloves. His hunting gloves. She knew what that meant. "You won't shoot me," she said defiantly. "If you wanted to kill me, you would have done it a long time ago."

"I should have," said Alex. "You wanted my family dead. You went to great lengths to have it accomplished. You are a clear and present threat to my family."

"You won't kill me. I'm your daughter."

"Leave now, Kari."

Kari began walking toward the door.

Cate actually smiled. "Why are you

playing like that? You won't shoot me. I'm your daughter."

Alex could hardly contain his rage and his pain. He lifted his gun. And he held it to his daughter's forehead.

Kari turned around as she stood at the door. Cate was staring at Alex, and he was staring at her. And he was trembling as he held that gun. Kari knew it was going to be the hardest thing he'd ever done. But she also knew it had to be done. Cate was not going to stop unless he stopped her.

And just as Kari turned to walk out, so that she didn't have to bear witness of what she knew was going to destroy a big part of her husband, a shotgun blast tore through the condo's downstairs window and caught Cate in the back of her head.

At first Kari and Alex both were shocked. They both had ducked. Until they realized Cate had been shot.

Cate, at first, began to wobble with a look of amazement on her face. She was thunderstruck, as if it couldn't be happening to her. Then she looked at her father and fell against him.

Kari hurried back into the living room as Alex eased his daughter to the floor with his hand on the back of her head. When he lifted his hand, it was covered in her blood. Kari quickly checked her pulse. She looked at Alex and shook her head.

Then Alex hurried over to the shattered window, with Kari hurrying behind him. They saw, across the street, an SUV. Then they saw Mick Sinatra as he pulled his rifle back inside of the vehicle. He looked at them as they stood at that shattered window. He stared at them. And then he pressed up the window of his own SUV, and then his driver drove him away.

Tears streamed down Kari's face. She was so grateful that Alex wasn't forced to have the blood of his own daughter on his hands that she could hardly contain herself. Mick the Tick did it for him because family came first with that man. He was a lot of things. But Alex was right. He was a family man above all else.

They looked at each other. Alex turned and looked at his daughter on that floor. And he staggered back. She was gone. Finally she was gone.

And he said a mouthful. "The bitch is gone," he said, as he stared at her.

It was a terrible thing for a father to say about his own child. And Kari couldn't agree with him more.

She took charge, and called for a cleanup crew.

EPILOGUE

"Is it going to be scary, Daddy? Jordan says it's going to be scary."

"Don't listen to your brother. It won't be scary at all. You'll love it."

"I told you, Jordan. Daddy says I'll love it."

"They're like mummies who come to little girls bedrooms and snatch them away in the middle of the night," Jordan joked, kidding with his kid sister.

But Angela didn't like that kind of joke. "Quit playing with me," she said.

"Stop playing, J," said Alex. And it was only then did Jordan cut it out.

And then the lights went down in the movie theater and Alex, with Kari seated beside him, and Angela seated beside her, and Jordan on the end, enjoyed something as simple as a night out at the movies.

As the coming attractions appeared on screen, and as Jordan and Angela munched on their popcorn and enjoyed the previews, Alex placed his arm around Kari.

"You aren't bored, are you?" Kari asked him.

"Me? No way! A night out on the town with my family is what living's all about. It doesn't get any better than this."

"Thank you," Kari said.

"For what?"

"For choosing us."

Alex looked at her and pulled her closer against him. "That was the easiest choice of my life," he said. "I should be thanking you."

"For what?"

"For choosing me over Diallo."

Kari grinned. "I saw him yesterday."

Alex looked at her. He wasn't sure if he wanted to hear that. "Really?"

"He came by the office. You know what he said to me?"

"What?"

"He said after that tussle he got into with you, he phoned this private detective he has on payroll and told him it was now or never. That he had to find some smut on you, preferably involving another woman, so that it would give me a great reason to leave you and go to him.

ALEX DRAKOS: HOUSE ON FIRE

But he said he came to realize that no matter what you do, I wasn't ever leaving you."

Alex stared at her. "Is that true?"

"Faye and Lucinda would say it's dangerous to admit it," said Kari. "But yes, it's absolutely the truth."

Alex smiled a satisfying smile. "Same here," he said. "They will have to pry you from my cold, dead hands before I let you go."

Kari laughed, they kissed, and then they snuggled closer and enjoyed their popcorn and movie too.

Visit
www.mallorymonroebooks.com
or
www.austinbrookpublishing.com
for more information on all titles.

ABOUT THE AUTHOR

Mallory Monroe, a pseudonym of Teresa McClain-Watson, is the bestselling author of over one-hundred-and-sixty novels. Visit mallorymonroebooks.com or austinbrookpublishing.com for more information on all titles.

Made in the USA
Middletown, DE
01 June 2023

31904186R00170